UNDERTOW

by Alessandra Torre

UNDERTOW

In some ways, I was ordinary. Waking up in bed with Paul, our life filled with sandy toes and tan lines. I stocked books during the day and danced with him to Bob Marley at night.

In other ways, I was unordinary. I'd dust off the sand and step into Stewart's limousine. Zip up my evening gown and slide into my other life. Champagne and maid service. Orgasms and my businessman.

My life was a tide, pulling me back and forth between the two men. Soothing. Peaceful.

Then the undertow came, pulling my lives together, my men colliding, my breath shortening, arms flailing against the current, my heart breaking in its strength.

I should have known it would never work out.

Original Title: Sex, Love, Repeat

Edited: Madison Seidler (2013)

Proof: JO's Proofing, Erik Gevers

Cover: Perfect Pear Creative

OTHER BOOKS BY ALESSANDRA TORRE:

Erotic Romance:

Black Lies

Love Chloe

The Innocence Trilogy

Romantic Suspense:

Moonshot

Trophy Wife

Even Money / Double Down

Tight

The Deanna Madden Trilogy

Contemporary Romance:

Hollywood Dirt

Love in Lingerie

Hidden Seams

Romantic Comedy:

Tripping on a Halo

Contemporary Fiction:

The Ghostwriter

This book is for the girl with her head down,
and the inner strength I know she carries.

1

The heart is stubborn. It holds onto love despite what sense and emotion tells it. And it is often, in the battle of those three, the most brilliant of all.

"Madison."

I hear my name, but I cannot open my eyes. I try, pushing and pulling with the weak muscles of my eyelids, but there is no movement. Nothing to minimize the blackness, nothing to pull me from this rabbit hole of darkness. But I can hear. I have emerged into awareness with only one sense, and I grab onto it and pull upward, trying to raise myself into life through the elements of sound alone. I hear my name, hear Paul say it, crystal clear, his voice thick with emotion. I strain for more, worried he has left, tensing and pushing every muscle I have, trying for movement, trying to reach out with my hands and grab his skin, his shirt, anything.

Then I pause on my journey, all my efforts freezing, stalled in their worthless attempts, because a second voice has joined the first.

Stewart.

A voice I love—his deep, authoritative tone one that traditionally makes my breath quicken and my knees weak. But here, in this place, it makes my heart drop. His voice should never be heard in tandem with Paul's, their presences should never be intersected, much less raised in what sounds to be an argument.

And I know, as my mind closes off—pushes me deeper into the black hole of oblivion, my subconscious fighting tooth and nail as I am pulled down, down, down—I have failed. All of my attempts, my careful lives of separation ...

"Madison." I hear my name one last time, but it is so faint, I cannot tell which man it comes from.

THREE MONTHS EARLIER

2

DANA

I am nosy. A meddler. Mom used to say it would be my downfall. She was probably right. It certainly got me in enough trouble early in life, my matchmaking skills often falling flat, my snooping ending disastrously. As an adult, I should know better. I should keep to myself—keep my curiosity to a minimum.

I haven't seen Stewart in three years. Ever since we had a big blow up over Thanksgiving dinner and his inability to have time for anything but work. I now regret that fight. It was valid, and I was in the right, but it wasn't worth the silence. Silence that stretched a week, then a month, then years, each passing holiday a reminder of my loss. I don't know the reason for his silence. Is it stubbornness or the fact that his busy schedule has pushed thoughts of me out of his mind? I don't know what's worse—intentionally being snubbed or being forgotten about completely.

On my end, it was initially stubbornness, our commonalities peaking in that one trait: pride. And since I, after all, was right, there was really no reason for me to break first—to weaken and reach out when he was the one in error. Now, it doesn't really matter whether I was right. I just want him back. Sadly, my point has been proven even more by his silence. He doesn't have time for me. He only has time for work. And for *her*, that blonde who holds his busy heart in her hands.

I first saw them in the Los Angeles society pages, his hand tight around her waist, her smile bright and natural, affection in her eyes as she beamed at him. He is so rarely photographed, never having the time for the premieres or charity galas that most men of his position flock to like obedient animals. He doesn't lunch at the Ivy or stroll through Beverly Hills. He takes the elevator down from his condo, walks four buildings west, and rides a different elevator up to his office. Work. Sleep. Repeat. At least that was his life when I knew it, when I had a small part in his heart. Maybe things are different now. Maybe he takes weekends off, has dinner dates, movie nights, and tropical vacations, and takes that ray of California blonde right along with him.

But I doubt it. My online stalking has shown no such habits. Best I can tell, he is the same Stewart—*she* is the only change.

I haven't yet figured out if she's a passing fancy or a long-term possibility, but I'll find out. I moved here, in small part, to become a part of his life again, whether he wants me to or not. So, I'll find out more about her. Soon, I'll know how much of a role she plays in his life. I'll sit back, watch, and gather information.

He's certainly too busy to notice me watching.

3

HOLLYWOOD, CA

MADISON

I don't know what it is about a wealthy man that women find appealing, but I'm victim to it along with the rest. And Stewart wears wealth as well as any man I know.

The backdrop of finery complements him. His large frame settles into expensive leather chairs; crystal chandeliers cast dramatic highlights on the beautiful lines of his face, and ocean glitters off the brilliant blue of his eyes. His Patek Philippe watch glints, the edge of it barely visible under the cuff of his dress shirts. His custom suits move easily beneath my fingers, sliding over his broad shoulders, the hard definition of trained muscles rippling under pale skin. I've never seen him with a tan, his hours spent indoors, his workouts done under the muted lights of his penthouse gym and directed by a blonde bombshell named Tiffany.

Tonight, I only have to step inside, my entrance interrupting a set of pull-ups, his muscles popping as he suspends and lifts himself with easy efficiency. The additional light of the open door causes them both to turn, his eyes locking on mine with laser focus, and he drops lightly to his feet. "Tiffany," he says between hard breaths. "That'll be all."

I drop my bag as she hurries past, barely noticing the sound of her exit, my focus on Stewart, as he strides forward and grips my arms, lifting me easily and silently onto the counter, his lips pressing against mine quickly, before interrupting us with the cloth of my shirt, pulling it over my head and tossing it aside. He skips a greet-ing, focusing on my bare breasts, pressing me backward and taking a hungry mouth to my skin, his hands yanking and pulling on my shorts, sliding them down and off of my legs as his tongue plays a soft rhythm against my nipple.

He moves lower, tasting me, inhaling deeply between my legs. "God, you taste so good." He groans against my sex, his tongue dipping inside and fucking me thickly, his need pouring through his mouth and his hands, which caress my body like I am their final meal to feast on. He carries me to the bench and lays me down, his eyes dark and wild as he stares down at me, pulling down the cloth of his shorts until his cock pops free.

"This," he murmurs, "is going to be for me. I promise, I'll take care of you later."

I smile, spreading my legs apart and stretching out on the bench. His brand of fucking is relentless, strong thrusts in which he devours my body without restraint. It is what I have come here for —it's what I want. I need the domination, the edge of insanity that he barely holds in check. I need the madness in his eyes, the pure need that breathes through his body, the need only I can satisfy.

And there, on the leather bench, he rides us both to exhaustion.

I wake in his bed, two sheets between me and the down comforter, the soft voice of Estelle somewhere to my right. I roll over, blinking sleepily as her kind face comes into view.

"Are you ready for breakfast, Ms. Madison?"

"What time is it?" I prop myself up, holding the blanket against my bare chest.

"It's after ten, ma'am. Mr. Brand told me to wake you after—"

I nod, smiling slightly. "Yes. I didn't mean to sleep this long. What time did he leave?"

"Six-thirty ma'am."

I look around for my clothes, trying to trace back the moment when they had become victim to Stewart's hands. *His office.* "I asked you a year ago to stop calling me ma'am," I mumble, a yawn slipping out of my mouth.

"Yes, ma'am." She frowns regretfully, before starting over. "I'm sorry. Would you care for breakfast?"

"No, thank you. I've got to get going. My clothes from yesterday—"

"Were in the office. They have been washed and are hanging in your closet."

"Perfect. Thank you. Do you mind asking the valet to bring up my car?"

"Certainly. I'll be close by if you need me." She smiles brightly before backing into the hall and closing the suite's doors.

I yawn again, blinking the sleep from my eyes, and roll out of the bed. I walk into the granite-filled bathroom and turn on the steam shower.

4

VENICE BEACH, CA

I step from the bedroom a half hour later, jeans and a tank top on, my wet hair twisted into a bun. I swing by the kitchen on my way out, waving goodbye to Estelle and snagging a red apple and bottled water from the fridge.

I hop on Santa Monica Boulevard and move through lanes of traffic with ease, my car knowing the route as well as my soul, my thoughts wandering as I drive. The Audi was a gift from Stewart for my twenty-ninth birthday and was probably picked out by his assistant. Regardless of who chose the vehicle, I love it. White exterior, blood red leather inside, it is sleek, sexy, and just begs every degenerate in my neighborhood to steal it. I'm shocked it's survived the last five months.

It's fourteen miles between Stewart's home and mine, but it might as well be different countries. Stewart lives in the skyscraper world of downtown Hollywood, rarely leaving the blocks of the city unless jetting off for work. He works a hundred hours a week, sleeps six hours a night, and fucks the hell out of me the rest of the time. His needs are minimum: food, sleep, and sex. I take care of one of those. Estelle and his bed take care of the rest.

I get off on Lincoln Boulevard, the traffic lessening as frustrated drivers continue their trek along the freeway, anxious to continue their painful life. For a moment, I wish I'd put down the car's top, needing to feel the wind in my hair and hear the sound of the surf. Leaving Stewart's, I sometimes need a strong breeze to release the intensity he carries with him.

I pull off the road and turn down our street. Pressing the garage release button, I enter the dark space that is my spot and kill the ignition. I step out in the shadows, the overhead burnt out, Paul promising for the last five months to get around to it.

The steps are worn concrete, this townhome complex built before developers realized they shouldn't build shit housing this close to the beach. Property values in this area have hit ridiculous figures, and a six-figure income will still put you in the projects, dodging street beggars and used needles. We don't make six-figures. Paul brings in anywhere from fifty to sixty thousand surfing. I bring in far less than that, running a bookstore that operates out of a bar on Venice Beach. By California standards, it's practically poverty, but we don't need much. For Paul and I, we never have. We're lucky to have this place, my stepfather blessing us with a rent payment low enough to both piss our neighbors off and ensure that we can still cover food and utilities.

Paul and I met two years ago, at the Santa Monica pier, when we were side by side in the singles line for the rollercoaster. We had all of six minutes in line, the shuffle moving quickly, singles getting split up among the empty seats in a bored and orderly fashion.

He flashed a smile at me, and that was really all it took. Broad shoulders, tan skin that peeled a bit on his nose, and blue eyes that looked like a fucking turquoise magic marker. He was in board shorts, a T-shirt, and flip flops with muscular, track-free arms and no hint of tattoos. It was like God plucked an Abercrombie & Fitch model from the sky and injected him with testosterone and sexuality. I smiled back.

We spent those six minutes talking, our words spilling out between laughs and chemistry. I instantly liked him, had one of those at-peace realizations that he was a good guy. The type so good that women run over him, the type so good that he is often stuck in the friend-zone. But *this* guy? With his gorgeous looks and the I-will-fuck-you-in-this-line-right-now vibe? No woman was stupid enough to best friend this man. I wanted him, right there in that line, my panties sticking to me in the best way possible beneath my short cotton skirt.

We reached the front, our moment of separation, but were seated together, two of us in one bench, a ridiculous, never-should-happen moment, and I took the minute before liftoff to reach over and tug the back of his head toward me. His wide smile told me I wasn't crazy, that he wanted this every bit as much as I did. And I knew, in the moment our lips met, seeming to instantly know every part of the other's soul, that I would fuck him. I needed him inside me, needed his hands to grip my waist, his shirt to move off that beautiful chest and my bare breasts to replace it. I needed every inch of him against and inside of me. The rollercoaster bar jerked down, and we separated with a laugh.

"Ready?" he asked.

"Just prepare for screams." I grinned.

I was, and still am, a dramatic rider. I believe there's no point in doing something if you aren't going to do it with all of your heart. I raised my arms, I screamed bloody murder, and he loved every minute of it. We swept through the loading bay after one cycle, the operator amping the riders before pushing the button and letting us ride again.

The vibration of the seat underneath me, his leg brushing against mine, the anticipation of what was to come ... I attacked him as soon as the ride ended, grabbing his hand and tugging him out, the pounding between my legs reaching a fever pitch. I ran, pulling him along with me, our bodies weaving around families, couples, giant stuffed snakes, and dollar games of chance.

We broke from the crowd and moved faster, our flip-flops slapping against the wood boardwalk, the tinny laugh of children vaguely registering in my head. I broke right when I saw the opening and jogged down sandy steps, glancing behind me to make sure he was there. He was, his eyes bright and curious. "What are we ... where are we going?" he called out. I ditched my sandals when I hit the sea of white and ran through hot sand, gripping his hand and pulling him under the boardwalk, past a few homeless tents and down toward the water, where the posts are thicker, the cover more enclosed, privacy at a barely-there standard. I waded into calf-high water, pulling and then pushing him against a square post, my hands frantic on his shirt, my mouth fighting the movement of clothes for another chance at that gorgeous mouth.

His hands pushed my thin tee up over the curves of my bikini top, his firm fingers sliding the triangles of my bikini over and my breasts spilled free. His hands cupped and squeezed, his breath catching in my mouth. He pulled away, looking down, staring at my breasts in his hands before lifting them into the heat of his mouth. The sensation was incredible, his tongue soft yet firm, pliable against my delicate skin. I could feel him, hard against my thigh, and I reached back, digging into my pocket for what I always kept there—just in case. Just in case I met a man I couldn't resist.

He started at the touch of my fingers, dipping under the nylon of his shorts, and lifted off my breasts, surprised. "Here?" This close, I could see tints of green in his blue eyes, the color of ocean water, glittering brilliantly against the brown sand of his skin.

"Yes, here. I need you." I met his gaze confidently as I said the words, my hands already sealing the deal, pulling him out—*oh my god, hard*—and sliding protection over him with one smooth motion. His eyes darkened, intensity stealing over them, and he pushed me back against the wet wooden piling, pushing my skirt up as his hands gripped my ass and lifted.

Then I was in the air, his pelvis underneath me, supporting me against the post, and his fingers were skimming the line of my bikini bottoms, yanking the side tie loose. His mouth left mine, a gasp in his tone as his fingers pushed inside of me, one digit and then two. "Jesus. Are you sure?"

A stupid question as I hung before him, my breasts exposed, legs wrapped around his waist, my need dripping a path for his cock. "Give it to me," I breathed. "Hard."

He didn't ask again, didn't do anything but prop me hard against the piling and thrust. Quick strokes, his breath hard against my neck, his hands digging into the flesh of my ass, pulling and gripping the skin as he made his mark on my body. His fucks were wild, out of control, and I moaned against his neck, loving the fervor of his movements.

I cried out as I came and his mouth quickly moved to mine, muffling the sound as my body trembled, my legs squeezing his waist as intensity shook my body. It was too much, too great, the heat of my orgasm and clench of my sex, and I felt him as he came, the twitch and raw emotion that flowed through him, his breath gasping as he grunted, slowing his fucks and giving me a few final pushes.

"Oh my God," he whispered against my neck, his cock softening inside of me. "Oh my God. I think I'm in love with you."

He wasn't in love. Not yet. He was just surprised that a girl with perfect teeth and a bred-in-the-Valley smile would fuck a stranger under the Santa Monica Pier. And I thought, as I dropped to my knees in the water and peeled off the condom, taking him into my mouth and sucking the cum off his cock, that I would never see him again. That it would be that one fuckable moment and nothing else. But here we are, two years later and incredibly in love.

That's right. In *love*. Yes, I'm the same hoochie who got my brains fucked out on the weight bench. The one who has dated Stewart Brand, one of the most eligible bachelors in downtown Hollywood for the last two and a half years. I know what you're thinking. That dropped jaw and disgusted look on your face? I've seen it before. But wait. Please.

Don't judge me quite yet.

5

VENICE BEACH, CA

I am barefoot on the couch when Paul gets home, the door slamming open and shaking the wall art. I slide the headphones off my head and rise to my feet. "Hey lover," I say, wrapping my arms around his neck.

"Hey beautiful. How was life with the other half?"

"Bearable." I pull him tightly to me for a kiss. "I need you."

He welcomes me home with a kitchen fuck, my ass bare on the counter, legs wrapped tight around his waist. His mouth plays with my neck as he fucks, his pace smooth and unhurried, as if we have all the time in the world. And, in a way, we do. Nothing to do today, no appointments or places to be. He whispers dirty things as his hands slide around and beneath me, gripping my ass and pulling me into his strokes. My legs tighten around him, my walls constricting and squeezing, and his speed increases enough to take me over the edge and gently back down. Then, we move to the bed, him still hard and firm inside of me. There, on our worn sheets, he rolls me onto my side, and takes me to orgasm another two times, finishing with a groan.

ALESSANDRA TORRE

We lay entwined in each other's arms, a strong breeze of salt and sand blowing through the open window and over our damp skin. He pulls me closer and presses a soft kiss on my neck. "I love you, Madd."

"I love you, too." And I do. I love this man, who has not one stressed out bone in his body. He concerns himself with two things: surfing and keeping me happy. I love his outlook on life, a Bob Marley style philosophy. We fuck, we surf, and we love. There isn't too much else to our life. To this half of my life.

"Waves are supposed to be strong this afternoon. Wanna ride some today?"

"I think I'll hit the bookstore and log in a few hours. You go out this morning?"

"Yeah. Got up about five. Mavericks Invitational is in three weeks, so I'll hit it hard until then."

Paul doesn't need to practice. He is a god on a stick. His arms and legs work in perfect synchronization, his body gliding and bending at the perfect moment to stay balanced. Watching him surf makes my heart pound and my body clench. It is pure sex, the push and pull of muscles in a graceful movement that displays his athleticism. He's consistently ranked in the top twenty surfers in the world, a ranking that means little when it comes to his finances. Every competition is a negative investment, unless he wins. When he does win, sponsors are happy and prize money covers a few months of rent. When he loses, he's out his travel expenses, and we eat Ramen until the next big event.

I twist until my head is on his stomach, his hand beginning to run through my hair, pulling at bits of blonde and curling them around his fingers. I close my eyes, the movement soothing and familiar. Outside, some music starts up, the strands of reggae floating through the air and over our space. To Ziggy Marley's voice and against Paul's sun-kissed abs, I close my eyes and fall asleep.

16

6

HOLLYWOOD, CA

I hate society's notion that there is something wrong with sex. Something wrong with a woman who loves sex. I've loved sex for as long as I can remember. I lost my virginity at fourteen, when Gus Blankenship showed me his penis behind the gym, and I got so hot and bothered that I let him put it in me. We did it right there, with hard gravel digging into my back, his excited acne-covered face swinging above me. It was the best forty-two seconds of my life thus far.

That was back in the day when fourteen-year-olds were still pure, and not the makeup covered, push-up bra tramps they are today. Now, sixth grade sleepovers double as orgies where the girls fight over who's gonna get to suck the barely-handsome dad off first.

It's all wrong, the evolution of our innocent youth into cock-gobbling sluts. Which seems hypocritical coming from me, but it's not. I fuck because I love it, because I want to, because it brings me pleasure. They fuck because they think that they have to—for the guy, for the queen-bee girl, for the proverbial 'fuck you' to society that they imagine it creates.

They have it so backward, so twistedly screwed. Sex should be about mutual enjoyment, connection, the borrowing from another's fire at a moment when you want it most.

I pity them, with their glossy red lips and pierced belly buttons. Because, when it all comes to pass? When they 'grow up' and getting fucked during halftime is no longer cool but suddenly slutty? They will feel dirty, used and ruined. And all because they did it for the wrong reasons.

My phone rings, shrill and demanding. I sigh, the ringtone reserved for only one individual.

"Would you like me to get that?" The soft voice of the masseuse matches the dim room, soothing sounds, and eucalyptus scent.

"Do you mind bringing it to me? I'll put it on silent." I push up, taking the cell and silencing the call, flipping the button on the side to mute any future interruptions. "Sorry about that." I lay back down, holding out the phone, the woman taking it from me with a gracious smile.

It was my mother. I will need to call her back, as soon as Kindi finishes melting every muscle of my body. Paul needs this, to let this woman work her magic on his sore back and tight legs. But that will never happen. Kindi is a Stewart perk, her oiled hands rubbing me down in the spa of Stewart's skyscraper. Bringing Paul by would be combining my worlds, and as stupid as I am to have the two worlds, even I realize the danger in mixing their components. Overlapping cannot happen.

I take a deep breath and exhale, intentionally relaxing my shoulders, her fingers digging and pushing, breaking up a bundle of nerves, the pain excruciatingly pleasurable. I push all thoughts of Paul out of my head and focus on her hands.

7

HOLLYWOOD, CA

I grew up a charmed child of La Jolla. Nannies wiped my dirty ass, Christmas was spent in Aspen, and school uniforms shared closet space with miniature lines of Dior and Versace. I lived a privileged life between surfer chick and spoiled brat, sandy cheeks and wet bikinis chafing the leather seats of my ice blue BMW convertible. I smoked weed with friends in million-dollar mansions with ocean views while our parents cruised the Black Sea. I fucked preppy boys who wore Lacoste and Rolexes and played lacrosse. I was in a bubble of ridiculousness and grew up thinking that life never said no, credit cards were never declined, and happiness was a given.

Life was perfect until my father, a hedge fund manager with a minor addiction to cocaine, drove off the manicured edge of a Malibu cliff to the polished astonishment of a restaurant full of Orange County's upper society. His mistress, a surgically enhanced blonde three years older than me, was in the front seat, a fact which was hidden from no one, and embraced by many of my mom's arch enemies. They both died, killed by the cliffs.

In that moment, perfection became flawed and fragile.

Our money lasted another ten months until the fat mortgage, civil lawsuits, and attorneys took it all. I spent my senior year at the public high school, my BMW repossessed, my school uniforms left in the closet of a home that the bank quickly seized. I was unceremoniously dumped into normality alongside my mother, both of us immediately abandoned by our 'friends.'

Looking back, I see the turning point that occurred during that time. I miss my father. Despite his shortcomings and mistakes, I loved him, and can recognize bits of him throughout my personality. But the person that I was becoming? The type of individual bred by easy wealth and never-told-no parenting? I was a bitch. A self-assured, my-way-or-the-highway bitch. I didn't appreciate what I had and demanded more at every turn. I'm grateful that I got kicked in the ass and had a taste of reality before I traveled too far, and that persona became permanent.

My mother, on the other hand, was a lost cause. She was born and raised in those twenty thousand square foot mansions and handled middle-class life with the reluctance of an offended cat. She drowned herself in top-shelf martinis we couldn't afford, refusing to cook, clean, or pay bills—her breeding too far above such blue-collar work. I became the adult, she became the child, and our relationship dissolved until I moved out and she found a man. Now she is the wife and full-time dependent of Maurice Fulton, an old man who she can't possibly love, but one who keeps her groomed and outfitted in his big house and keeps her glass filled. I speak to her occasionally, when I get the sadistic urge to see what a society-bred alcoholic sounds like.

Isolation is one thing I have in common with my men. We are all loners, floating through life unattached, except to each other. We don't talk about our pasts and our lack of familial ties. There's no point in dwelling on the darkness, not when our life is full of such light.

Five months before Paul, I met Stewart on the street in downtown Hollywood. It was November and snowing. Not thick, heavy snow that allowed snowmen and powder fights, but a light flurry that swirled through the air and fell softly on open tongues, melting upon contact. It doesn't snow in our part of the world and the barely-there flurries were an event worth celebrating.

I was downtown, meeting my stepfather's attorney to sign some paperwork. Halfway through our meeting, I noticed the snow, and moved to the window, my hands and nose pressed to the glass like a child. I signed the final pages and ran down six flights of stairwell steps and burst into the frigid air.

I was spinning under the flurries, hands outstretched and face turned up to the sky, when I stumbled out of place and into the hard polish of his suit. He was walking, pausing only to right my stride before moving on. But my ankle turned in the stumble, and I let out a small cry of pain that had his eyes meeting mine, concern thick in his features. He stopped, gripping my arms, his stare intent on my face. "Are you all right?"

I winced, pushing against his chest and put some weight on my ankle, moving away from him and gripping the metal rod of a street sign. "I'm fine." I glanced up, watching the erratic swirl of flakes, my mouth curving back into a smile. "It's snowing!"

He dismissed the miracle of snow with one shrug of his suit. "Is your car close by?"

"It's just a few blocks up." I leaned against the pole, putting weight on my good foot. I held out my hand and watched as dots of white sprinkled my palm. I glanced over at him, momentarily distracted from the snow as I took in the gorgeous stranger. He had a custom suit stretched across a strong, tall build. Black hair, swept back and dotted with snow. Blue eyes staring at me with a mixture of impatience and concern. I smiled. "I'm good, really."

He sighed, then stepped closer, holding out his arm. "May I ... please? Let me carry you inside. I can have a driver take you home."

I laughed. "And not be able to get back to my car? That is thoughtful, but driving won't be a problem, it's my other foot."

He moved closer, his hand brushing my arm, and I started at the contact, the brush of touch electric. "Then I'll carry you to your car. Please." His eyes softened, the urgency in them gone, and I relaxed.

"If you insist." I smiled, giggling when he scooped me up. Cradling me to his chest, his intense eyes stared bemusedly down at me.

"This is funny?" he questioned, a flow of minty fresh breath floating down on me.

"Quite romantic, actually."

His hands supported me easily, my weight not slipping and sliding through his arms. I leaned in, resting my head against the wool of his suit, the bump of our movement slightly rocky. "Take a right here. It might be a hair more than a few blocks." I discreetly inhaled, a delicious blend of vanilla and forest hitting my nose, and I burrowed my face further into his chest.

"What's your name?" The words vibrated through his chest, and I lifted my head, staring at the strong muscles of his neck, and had the insane urge to lift my mouth to them, to trail playful kisses up, until I reached the fine shadow of his jaw, over that strong feature and to those lips.

I swallowed. "Madison. Decater."

He stopped walking, the abrupt change causing instability, my arms gripping his shoulders for balance, then snaking around his neck. He looked down, smiling, the bright flash of white teeth against the stubble of his five-o'clock shadow breathtaking. "Stewart Brand. It's a pleasure to meet you."

"Same here."

He then asked me where I lived and what I did. We laughed over his lack of book knowledge and his admission of no social life. We flirted, his hands tightened, and we walked two blocks past my car before I realized it and made him turn around.

We parted awkwardly, neither one of us wanting to step away, then his cell rang, and he glanced at his watch, muttering a curse. He passed me a business card while stepping away, answering the phone and bringing it to his ear.

"Call me," he mouthed. "Please."

Then he winked at me and left, talking quickly, his steps turning into a jog as he headed back up the street. I hobbled into the car and watched him disappear, waiting to see if he would glance back. But he didn't, and I stuffed his card into my purse and left, my tender ankle almost causing my Suzuki to sideswipe an adjacent Mercedes.

I sat on the card for a week, occasionally pulling it out and running my fingers over the surface. Women shouldn't call men. We should be pursued, should play the offhand, casual game until the men tackled us to the ground with flowers and affection. But his hurried exit, the urgency on his face when the phone rang, didn't give us the customary time to find pen and paper and exchange numbers. I bent the card slightly in my hand and considered tossing it in the trash to end the dilemma.

I didn't. Day nine, I called, an efficient female taking down my information in a manner that guaranteed no call back. Day ten, she called back, five times friendlier and set a lunch appointment for Stewart and I, three weeks later. I repeated the date uncertainly, expecting for her to be mistaken, and her cheerful tone hardened slightly as she informed me that he was a very busy individual, and she had shifted an entire day to accommodate that time frame. I took the date. Thirty months later, I don't need her to shift schedules. I get my stolen time in the middle of the night, or during a business dinner, or if an appointment cancels and I am in the area to grab a quick bite or a fuck on his desk.

Snow. Falling snow is what brought us together. That and his hurried life, which collided us in the first place.

8

VENICE BEACH, CA

HARPOONING: [VERB]

COPPING WOOD WHILE SURFING.

I am woken in the night, a hand on my shoulder, shaking me gently. "Maddy." Soft lips brush my neck, the rough scruff of unshaven skin tickling my cheek.

I roll, pulling up on the sheet, the cool night air cold on my bare chest. "Stop," I mumble.

"Come on," Paul whispers, sliding under the sheet, the warm heat of his skin settling over mine, his weight gently supported by his knees and arms. The hot nip of his lips travels up my stomach and over my breasts before settling on my lips.

"I'm sleeping," I whisper between long kisses as his body settles deeper, pinning me to the bed, my legs spreading and wrapping around him.

"No, you're not." He grins, pulling the blanket over both of our heads, his face close in the darkness.

"Yes," I reply firmly. "I am." I reach between our bodies and adjusts his cock so it lies against his stomach in a position which will better stimulate me when it hardens. He grinds slightly against me and I tighten my grip, feeling the reaction in his cock, the thickening.

"I like you when you sleep." He leans down, taking a long taste of my mouth and slowly thrusts his pelvis, the firm friction right *there* against my clit as it should be. I release his cock and wrap my arms around his neck. "Waves are at eight feet," he says against my mouth, a flash of teeth shining in the darkness.

"So ride them."

"I'd rather ride something else right now."

"Me too."

I don't need to move his cock. His hips take care of that, a small downward shift and his hardness makes the transition easy, my wet entrance more than ready for fulfillment. He resumes his strokes, slow and perfect inside me. The air under the blanket heats.

Strokes quicken.

I pant.

The bed shakes.

My heels dig into his back.

"Don't stop..." I beg.

I yank the blanket off his head, frantic for the cool air as we both arch into the darkness of oblivion.

I dress, slipping on bikini bottoms and a surf shirt, linking my hand through his and jogging down the garage steps. We grab our boards and move, quiet through dark streets, nodding to the familiar faces of homeless and beggars, the world that never sleeps, discomfort or addiction keeping them awake. When our feet hit the sand we run, eager to fly.

The water is frigid, and I fully wake up, paddling out into the darkness, following the glint of Paul's board. We ride until the waves calm, then we lay back on salty boards and watch the sun rise, reflecting sparks of fire across the tops of ripples.

You don't understand the true awesomeness of nature until you watch the sun rise on water that stretches across half the world. Or until you lay back on the board in the pitch black of night and listen to the world sleep. Until you feel the tug of water and know that you are dancing with a partner that could dip you into death should it feel the need. It is intoxicating, the heartbeat of the ocean. It flows through my blood; it sucks at my heart and pumps breath through my lungs.

I hear Paul's call and turn, realizing that he is already halfway in, waiting for me. In an hour, the crowds will come, hordes of tourists who have traveled across the country to play in our backyard. I roll to my stomach and paddle toward him.

9

HOLLYWOOD, CA

SPEEDBUMP: [NOUN]

SOMEONE WHO STANDS IN THE WAY OF A GOOD RIDE.

DANA

Some might call my behavior stalking. I'm of the opinion that, if you love the person, it gives you some justifiable leeway. My behavior this evening ... leeway doesn't really excuse it. It's border-line creepy. I sicced my assistant on Stewart. Told her I'd give her two hundred dollars for each event where she could reasonably predict his presence. It took her three weeks, but she found one. His business partner's birthday party at Livello on Friday night. She called the restaurant, verified that the reservations were at nine o'clock that evening, and we discussed the chances of him being present. A hundred percent chance of him being invited, and we were thinking a twenty-five percent chance of attendance. I was grasping that narrow percentage with the tenacity of a drowning woman.

It's ten, and I am huddled in the back corner of the lobby, nursing a bottled water, a gossip magazine held open before me. My mission is simple. If he is alone, approach him. And if he is with someone, scope her out. I'm giving myself 'til eleven, then I'm going to toss Belinda her two hundred bucks and go home to soak my feet in Epsom salts. I curse the three-inch heels I put on this morning and vow to wear flats on my next stakeout.

The door opens, and in a burst of cool air and perfume, they enter.

God, three years hasn't changed him. He is smiling, and that is the first thing I notice. Holding the door open for her, his hand moves to cup her waist when she moves through the door in front of him. Their cheeks are flushed, her giggle reaching back into the dark corner where I sit, a curl of jealousy snaking through me at the sound. I sink in my seat, watching them closely and noticing everything. The brush of his hand against her ass, the look in his eyes when she grabs the fabric of his shirt and presses into his chest, his head dipping down for a kiss. They are quickly escorted into the restaurant, away from my eyes, and I strain for a final glimpse of him, blocked by the Maître d'.

I exhale, setting down the magazine and lean back in my seat with a heavy sigh. I pick up my purse. There is no point in staying to see them leave. I saw everything I needed in that brief moment. The look in his eyes ... she is not a fling. Not an escort who he hires for events. *That* was the look of love.

My hands tighten around my clutch.

10

2 YEARS EARLIER

MADISON

It didn't take long for Stewart and I to fuck. The sweet circum-stance of our meeting quickly turned to heat, chemistry sizzling across the linen tablecloth of our first date. For the second date, two weeks later, I told his icy secretary I'd meet him at his place, intent on putting the little time she had penciled in to good use. She extended the appointment, giving me a full two hours, which I took as a good sign. Two weeks later, I handed my keys to a freckle-faced valet, signed in with the security desk at Stewart's condo, and was yanked inside the moment he opened the door.

He crab-walked me backward and I reached for his face, pulling it to mine, our first kiss frantic. "Tell me if I'm reading this wrong," he rushed out between kisses. "Is this too fast?"

I bit back a laugh, unbuttoning the front of my shirtdress and drop-ping the material to the floor, nothing but bare skin underneath. "You tell me, is it?" I stepped away and his eyes devoured me, his expression turning dark, his hand running roughly through his hair.

Then his mouth and his hands were on me. We started against the wall with frantic kisses as I yanked at his shirt, belt and pants until he was naked before me. My breath caught at his build. He was a tight coil of muscles that all seemed to center and point on a package that would have made my first boyfriend duck his head in shame. Stewart lifted me, my legs wrapping around his waist, and carried me to a bedroom.

I didn't notice the heated floors or the custom blinds or the ten-thousand-dollar rug. I only noticed the heat of our bodies, the perfect fit, the exact blend of control and fury that took my body from above, behind, and from below.

Forty-five minutes after I set foot in his condo, he straddled me. Breathing hard, his face tight in concentration, his hands running over the skin of my breasts, he leaned forward and kissed me, pushing away my hands when I reached for him. His cock bobbed between us, brushing my stomach, a plastic slap of latex against my skin. "Don't," he groaned. "I'm too close. Give me a moment."

But I was high on orgasms and anxious to see the result of our work. I smiled at him and slid the condom off, exposing his slick head. I worked my hand up and down as I watched him.

He squeezed his eyes tight, his breath coming out in short spurts. "I can't, you're—" He bucked his hips, groaning my name. I quickly jerked his shaft, watching in excitement as he released multiple shots on my chest. His head dropped back as he finished, a long sigh releasing. He collapsed to the side, his limbs heavy on the bed, his eyes closed, a smile on his face.

I rolled, unmindful of the sheets, and rested my head on his bicep, relaxing.

Minutes passed with no sound other than our breaths and the whip of the fan, neither of us feeling the need for compliments or unnecessary conversation.

Then he rolled to his side and studied me. "How are you single?"

I shrugged. "I don't need a boyfriend."

"Women rarely need the things they want." He ran his fingers gently along the inside of my arm.

"I'm not exactly normal," I offered. His mouth curved at the words, light entering them, a sarcastic response on the tip of his tongue. I waved his comeback off. "I don't mean that in a good way. You and I? Having sex so quickly? It wasn't because of your penthouse or your gorgeous blue eyes. It was sex, great sex, but just for pleasure. What we just did ... I'm not expecting anything from you because of it. I don't need to make 'this' anything more than what it is right now."

He frowned. "So you want to use me ... you *are* using me. For sex."

I laughed. "Oh, please, it's every man's perfect scenario. Don't give me that guilt trip."

His frown twitched slightly at the corners. "And what if I want more?"

"I don't think you have time for more."

From the start, I knew what I was signing up for, and I made sure he knew the same. I was a sexual creature and wouldn't stand by and wait to be beckoned. So, I lived my normal life, with bits of Stewart's cock sprinkled in when he had time. And that lasted for a bit, until he started getting attached and decided he didn't want me screwing strangers any more.

11

2 YEARS EARLIER

"I want you to find a boyfriend," Stewart said gruffly, while I was pinned against the wall of his office, his rigid cock inside of me. It was nine o'clock on a Tuesday night and everyone with any sanity was gone, save a uniformed cleaner who'd already stuck his head in and caught us in the act.

"What?"

He thrust upward, the depth making me ache. "A boyfriend. Someone to fuck you when I am busy, someone who can take you on dates and rub your feet and listen to you talk about your day."

"I already fuck when you're busy." The statement caused his eyes to darken and his thrusts increased in force and speed.

It wasn't new information, he knew I wasn't exclusively his. It was a choice he made, his addiction to success and files and stock prices too time-consuming to allow for more than a night or two a week with me. And our time together was often like this—squeezed in at a time when stress lined his face, and meetings or emails were only a step or two away.

"I don't like you screwing a bunch of strangers. It's not safe. And you deserve more than that."

I wished he would stop talking. The words were halting his movement, his serious expression putting a damper on my arousal. "Let's discuss this later."

He continued on, ignoring my suggestion. "You deserve someone who will be there for you. Who will take you on dates and watch out for you. Take you to the doctor when you're sick."

"So you want me to ditch you for someone with more time?"

He scowled and lifted me up, my arms wrapping around his neck for security, as he carried me across the room and deposited me on his desk. "Fuck no. I will never allow someone to take you from me." He ran his hands possessively over my front, pulling up my tank top and caressing the bare breasts beneath, his hands firm and strong, cupping my breasts like he owned them. I sighed when he dropped his face down and took one in his mouth. "But I don't want to lose you because you need time and affection. Get an everyday man to satisfy those needs." He met my gaze as his pace resumed, that dark glitter of intensity that I loved returning to his eyes. "But I will always own your heart. And he'd be second to me there."

I smiled, wrapping my legs around his hips and squeezing. "You can't control my heart, Stewart."

He lowered himself to me, bending over the desk as he thrust and withdrew with deep, possessive fucks. Gripping my arms and pinning them to the desk, he took a long, deep taste of my mouth before breaking away and staring into my eyes. "I can sure as hell try."

I closed my eyes, gripping his hips, and let him fuck me through another two orgasms before he came in my mouth, his eyes glued to mine as he pumped himself onto my tongue. I thought he would drop the 'boyfriend' talk—assuming it was mid-sex ridiculousness that would never be spoken of again. But he pressed the issue, revisiting the topic enough times that I realized his sincerity. He worried about my safety and happiness. Stressed over losing me due to lack of attention. He wanted me to have a steady fuck, wanted someone to make up for the slack he couldn't provide. He wanted someone safe and friendly, someone I wouldn't leave him for, but that would make me happy.

He wanted Paul, I just hadn't found him yet.

So, I continued screwing strangers, my libido as aggressive as ever. Valet boys with pretty hair. Businessmen at bars. Sunburnt tourists on Venice Beach.

And then, on that day in Santa Monica, I met Paul.

I fucked Paul.

And he was different. As he stared into my eyes and fucked me in the surf, Paul was someone Stewart would approve of.

Safe.

Friendly.

Sweet.

Paul has changed since that day. He's more possessive of me than he once was, his cock claiming me as if he has something to prove. He is not safe, and Stewart has every cause to be worried. They both own my heart now, an equal division fought over by two sets of blue eyes.

12

VENICE BEACH, CA

My phone rings and I glance at it. LOVER displays across its front. *Stewart*. I opened the phone. "Hey babe."

"Hey. You free Thursday night? I have a work thing ... need a date."

"Sure."

"Perfect. I'll connect you to Ashley." There is a click and a few tones before the cheerful voice of his assistant fills my ear. We chat for a few minutes, and then I hang up.

"Was that him?" Paul continues his slow patient swipes of wax protection, across the surface of his bright red board. We are in the garage, the door up, our cars pulled into the alley. Every few minutes, bikers pass through the open space. I've already waxed my board, my job quickly and haphazardly done with no real care. But Paul takes his time and stretches the task out, his eyes careful, his strokes sure and familiar.

"Yeah. I've got a thing to attend tomorrow night. I'll be back in the morning. When do you leave for Costa Rica?" I watch his shoulders for tension, his jaw for rigidity, but he is calm, peace in his eyes, an easygoing manner in his movements.

"End of next week. I'll be gone four or five days, depending on the flight." He sets down the wax, walking around the board and leans against my car, pulling me by the waist, into his arms. "I'm gonna miss you, Madd."

I smile, leaning into his chest. "I'll be here when you get back."

"Promise?"

"Promise." I lift my chin, and he kisses me, his mouth greedy. This is Paul's worry, that one day he'll return and I will be gone. He's afraid I will choose Stewart and not him.

He doesn't mind sharing, but losing me terrifies him.

I flip through book titles, pulling out spines and sliding in new ones, running over the alphabet in my head, making sure that everything was in its proper place, J.D. Robb sitting after James Patterson and before Nora Roberts. I feel him before I see him, the creak of the floor behind me announcing a visitor's weight, the air carrying the scent of sunscreen and sweat.

I don't pause, intent on filing these last three books before my mind gets sidetracked, and I have to start the whole damn alphabet again.

"You know ebooks are going to replace these pretty soon." Paul's confident drawl sounds, and I smile despite my best attempt to keep a cool exterior.

I squeeze the last book into place and turn to face him. "Easy— words like that'll get you killed around here."

He scoffs, crossing his tan arms across a broad chest, covered in a blue Billabong tank. "You don't have a dangerous bone in your body."

I walk around the rack of books between us, until I stand in front of him. "You're right about that. I'm in sore need of a dangerous bone inside of me."

He groans and his eyes turn from playful to feral in a moment, as he reaches out and pulls me tight to him. I can feel his pelvis tilt, our fit tight enough that the ridge of his erection digs into me. He lets out a shuddering breath as he lowers his mouth to mine. "You want me to fix that situation?"

"Oh yeah." I grin, reaching up and tugging his head down, exploring the taste of his kiss as he pulled me closer.

"I want to fuck you right here," he whispers.

"So do it." My hands slip under his shirt, trailing over the lines of his abs, his breath catching as I get one hand into the low waist of his board shorts, my fingers encountering the curly patch of hair there.

He chuckles and pulls my hand out, planting a kiss on the top of my head. "I'll take care of you later. I just wanted to stop in and say hi."

I let out a dramatic sigh, wilting against the bookshelf. "*Fine*. I'm closing up shop at four. Meet you on the beach?"

He cradles my face, his gaze trailing over my features. "I'll be there. Tonight is when you have that thing?"

I nod. "I'll be back in the morning."

He grins, my playful boy back. "Then I'll be sure to take care of you this afternoon."

I yank him forward. "You better."

He gives me a final kiss before releasing me, tossing out a carefree smile before ducking through the entrance and disappearing into the bright California sun.

I understand that you may hate me. That you may curse me for my greed. But if I'm okay with it, and they're okay with it, how is it anyone else's right to judge me?

13

VENICE BEACH, CA

CAVEFISH: [NOUN]

PALE SURFER

DANA

I stub out my cigarette and watch the bar, listening as my coworker blabs the explicit details of last night's blind date. I tune in occasionally, nodding politely and cracking a smile when the occasion seems to call for it. But mainly, I just watch the bar. *I saw her. Stewart's blonde princess.* I was sitting here, minding my own business, sipping fresh coffee and munching on biscotti when she trotted by. Flashing a smile to a pothead who sat on the curb, she entered the bar without a second glance around. That was forty-five minutes ago.

I light another cigarette.

Venice Beach... it wasn't the location I expected to find her in.

From my first impression at Livello, she had seemed too upscale for this area—her glowing skin and sparkly white teeth speaking of good breeding, the dress one that appeared to be four-figure fabulous. I almost didn't recognize her in cutoff shorts and a plaid, long-sleeved button-up, aviators perched on her head, long tanned legs ending in a pair of leather flip-flops. But it's hard to miss a girl like her. And I've thought about that night too many times, replaying it over and over again in my head.

Stewart had barely aged, one hundred percent the man I knew—save the grin on his face. That grin, the glint in his eyes... all signs of a man in love. Sadly, I didn't have much experience with being on the receiving end of those.

I take a sip of coffee. Yep, Venice Beach is certainly not where I expected to find her. Then again, who am I to talk about being in random places? I'm sitting here in a wool suit and sweating my ass off, all in the slim hope that I might run into Paul.

Paul. The other man in my heart, and also MIA in my life. His absence pulls at my soul. Paul, the lost lamb of our family. What happened to Jennifer wasn't his fault. Things happen regardless of our best intentions and precautions. Things happen, and when disaster struck, we lost him. He was always too sensitive, too caring, too loving. Quick to accept blame when it wasn't cast on him, quick to perceive if someone was mad or if feelings were hurt. He carried the happiness of our family on his shoulders, as if his young frame could support so much pressure. And that summer was a bomb to that structure, a heavy cannonball dropped onto a frail teenager's house of sticks.

We should have known he wouldn't recover. We should have known it would push him away. Now, he lives as if that event never happened. As if Jennifer, and the rest of us, never existed.

I think the mere presence of us causes him pain. We're nothing but a walking billboard of what used to be. So, he pretends we aren't here and walks through life with a smile on his face.

I don't know if that makes me happy or sad. I'm relieved that he's okay. In press photos, his grin stretches wide and easily. Tournament videos show that his step has a bounce in it. But I'm sad for the brother I've lost, one who seems like he will never return home.

"I feel like three days is too long. If he hasn't called by then, fuck him, you know?" Shannon shrugs, then looks to me for approval.

I nod. "Agreed. Fuck him."

She started back in, and I glanced in the direction that the blonde had gone, then did another sweep of the restaurant for Paul. He lives around here somewhere. I don't have his number, can't find anything but a manager's contact info on the promotional website bearing Paul's stage name. The alias irks me, a visible sign indicating his separation from our family. *Linx*. It was a stupid last name, picked by a nineteen-year-old kid with more pussy and dreams than he knew what to do with.

I exhale a burst of smoke and glance towards the beach. YouTube videos show him here—attacking waves with the same ferocity he exhibited as a kid. So, when Shannon wanted some gossip time, I suggested Venice Beach, hoping that fate would be on my side.

I take a sip of coffee and glance at my watch, my mind bouncing off Paul and back to the surprise sighting of Stewart's blonde. It'd been fifty-two minutes. Who sits in a bar at two o'clock on a Monday afternoon for almost an hour? I push back from the chair and Shannon pauses mid-sentence, looking at me with surprise. "Where're you going?"

"Just a minute," I mutter, throwing my bag over my shoulder and zig-zagging through the crowd. I pull on the handle and step into the bar.

A woman should be dressed properly to go into battle. But I wasn't expecting to confront Stewart's Barbie doll this morning. I was only hoping to see Paul, and wore an outfit he would recognize me in. While I'd dressed, I had envisioned the moment he saw me. His eyes would light up, and he'd toss an arm over my shoulder, a soft kiss placed on my cheek. And in that moment, everything would be perfect. He would understand I still love him, that I will always love him—no matter what. And he would tell me that he loves me and would invite me to be a part of his life once again.

So I wore a suit, my normal skin. It would stand out on the boardwalk, and might cause Paul to take notice and recognize me. But now, walking into the bar filled with flip-flops and tan bodies, I wish I had at least worn my good heels. Prada would help me have the confidence to approach this woman. Prada would hold my hand and whisper in my ear that I am cool enough, hip enough, to approach this woman who is probably ten years my junior.

My eyes take a moment to adjust to the dark, neon lights coming into focus, the floor beneath my heels sticky. Only two figures are at the bar, neither of which are her. The bartender, a redheaded pixie who should have worn sunscreen earlier in life, raises her chin at me. "What'cha need?"

My palms are suddenly clammy, and I wipe them on the front of my skirt, trying to think of some plausible need for my presence. "Do you have a restroom?"

She pops her gum with a crude, loud crack. "It's outside, past the bookstore. Down that hall." She points at a dingy hall, just past an open doorway with glossy paperbacks stacked on either side of the door. Curiosity makes my gaze linger and the reggae music from inside draws me closer to the hall.

An arm snakes out the door, startling me. It is low, from the height of a small child, and pushes a heavy hardcover out the door until it bumps into an adjoining stack. I move forward, peering in, and see Stewart's blonde sitting cross-legged on the floor, books stacked all around her. *She works here.* The realization that she is not a barfly is relieving. I step back, but not before her head snaps up, and our eyes meet for one terrifying moment.

She smiles. "Please don't leave. I can turn the music off if it bothers you."

"Oh no, it doesn't bother me." I brush aside a stray hair that's come loose from my bun, trying to find my mindset. Why had I come looking for her? What was my ball-busting plan of attack? Suddenly, my lack of designer shoes seems to be the least of my poor planning. "I was just looking for the bathroom."

She frowns, and it's such a ridiculously adorable gesture that I want to throttle her. "Damn. I was hoping for a reader. It's been crickets today." She stands, brushing off her shorts and leaving the pile of books behind. "Want me to show you the way?"

"No, it's okay." I glance around the small space. It's just a few rows squeezed into an area lined with floor-to-ceiling shelves, shiny new books squeezed next to worn paperbacks with broken spines.

"Oooh... I know that look. What's your weakness? Steamy billionaires with foot-long junk? Or a serial killer taking out half the women in Mississippi?" She shoots me a wicked grin.

I blush, hating the fact that I'm fighting off a smile. This is not how this is supposed to go. She shouldn't be likable. I had expected upper crust, snooty, perfectly manicured fingers digging as far into Stewart's money pile as they could possibly go. "Janet Evanovich."

"Oooh! I knew I liked you." She jogs past me, humming along with the music as she drags a stool over to a shelf and stands, stretching up and trotting her fingers over titles. "You want the latest?"

"Sure."

"Have you read Stephanie Bond?"

I watch her carefully, trying to pick up more clues. "Uhh ... no."

She jumps off the stool, crouching down briefly and skims over a second shelf, snatching a book from the rack and tilting her head toward the register. "Anything else before I ring you up?"

I shake my head, reaching into my jacket pocket for some cash.

She rounds the tiny register desk and taps at the keys. In this light, I can see that she's a natural blonde, her hair wild and windblown, the tips of her cheeks a little burnt. It's funny, if I had seen this version of her first, I would have pictured her with Paul, but not Stewart. It was hard to pair this reggae listening beach bum with the sleek and sophisticated woman who had beamed up at Stewart.

"If you like Evanovich, you gotta check out Bond, too." She held up the second book. "It's used, so I'm gonna toss it in no charge. Just ignore the worn pages. She is freakin' awesome." She shrugs, then stuffs it into a bright green bag. "Just check it out."

I smile, counting out bills and passing them over. "Thank you—I will."

She walks around the counter and hands me the plastic bag with a smile. "Thanks for coming in. You want me to show you to the bathroom?"

Oh, right. My imaginary need to pee. I shake my head. "I'm good. Thanks for the book."

I take a right out of the store, walking down the dim hall and lock myself in the dirty bathroom. I stand in the middle of the germ-infested space, trying not to touch anything, and wait. Two minutes later, I use a paper towel to flush the toilet and open the door handle. I avoid looking into the bookstore, walking quickly through the dark bar and back into the bright light. The high-top where I sat with Shannon is empty, a pink post-it stuck to her spot, an intense frowny face drawn on it in blue ballpoint pen. I glance around but see no sign of her. Sighing, I crumple the sticky note, dump my coffee into the trash, and cast one final look for Paul before leaving.

14

VENICE BEACH, CA

MADISON

For the next two years and three months, I'm sterile. Then it will be time to pull out the hormone implant in my arm and replace it with a fresh one, and I can make that humongous decision again.

To have a baby or not have a baby.

It was an easy decision a couple of years ago. But... I'm already waffling. In two years, I'll probably be beside myself with the hefty choice. In a way, choosing a baby will be like choosing between my boys. It'll be a conversation I'll have to have with both of them, and I can already guess their stances on it.

Stewart won't have time for a child and will tell me so without hesitation. He'll support any financial obligation, but anything more... I'll be on my own.

On the other side, Paul will ask what makes me happy. And whatever I say, he'll go with. It's how our relationship has always been. He does what makes me happy. It is why he accepts the fucked-up relationship dynamic that we currently have.

While Stewart wants me to have a second man to keep me off the streets, to keep me from being lonely, to keep me in his life—Paul accepts that I have a second man because it was what he signed up for. He'd rather have half of me than none of me.

But he didn't always accept it so easily. The first time I brought it up, he left.

Two years ago.

After Paul's and my experience under the Santa Monica Pier, we had an official first date—meat lovers pizza under the dim lights of Joe's, cold beers downed, our bare legs brushing under the slanted brick bar top, knowing smiles paired with flirtatious looks.

I thought that'd be it, but he persisted, getting my number and calling the next day. I played coy, but he showed up at the bookstore and feigned interest in Gillian Flynn until he snagged a second date.

He didn't have to work too hard. I knew who he was, had wandered down to the beach after Bip went oh-my-God-that's-Paul-Linx crazy, spilling words like 'surfing god' and 'sweetheart' as if he was *onceinalifetime* special. I sat on the edge of the surf, sand sticking to my thighs, and watched him on his board, watched the speed and dare of his ride, and let my mind wander down the what-if road.

What if I went on a second, then third, then fourth date?

What about Stewart?

What about his idea of a second boyfriend?

Could I bring up that scenario? And if I did, how would Paul respond?

I watched him, admired the flex of muscles as he emerged from the gully of a wave, his gaze catching on me, recognition in his eyes. Then he waved, the smile broadening, and I waved, and I knew I would have to try.

I broached the subject on our fourth date. At that point, I was already a little too attached to his quick smile and always-ready cock. I waited until after sex, when we were stretched out on his bed, his hand running gently down the line of my back, the room quiet, save our contented breaths.

"Bring many girls here?" I teased.

He reached over, dragging me atop him until my head rested on his chest, my bare breasts on his stomach. "Not since I met you."

"Well, that's an impressive feat," I joked. "Seeing as we've screwed in this bed ... What? Three of the last four days?" I pushed up and crawled forward, straddling him. "So... there aren't any girlfriend's clothes hanging in that closet?" I tilted my head to the door—an accordion-style set that was half-blue, half-white.

He stretched back his arms, locking them behind his head and studied me, his face serious. "Why would you be here if I had a girlfriend?"

I shrugged. "Maybe she's busy. Out of town." His gaze follows me, staying on my face. "Maybe she doesn't care."

"I wouldn't be with someone if they didn't care," he said softly.

I'd been tracing the lines of his chest, his shoulder muscles enhanced by his position. I refocused my attention on his eyes, struggling to broach the unspeakable topic. "Because, I have someone..."

His abs tensed underneath me, his expression growing wary.

"Someone I date—it's not an exclusive thing." I rushed out the words, watching his features relax a bit. "He doesn't care. I mean, he *cares*, but he doesn't mind me dating other people. He's too busy for a full-time relationship."

"And?"

I grimaced and pulled the band-aid off with one, painful rip, anxious to get it off and move the hell on. "This guy, he's a part of my life. I love him. I just wanted to put it out there. I don't know what you're looking for, if it's a fuck buddy or—"

"I want a relationship," he interrupted me, his expression unreadable, and I fidgeted slightly on his hips.

It was too early to ask him the question, but I was already there, and he was waiting. Waiting while I was treading water, trying to figure out whether to dive deeper or swim for shore. Wondering if Stewart was worth this headache, while knowing, before my mouth even opened, that he was. "With me? I know it's early to ask that, but—"

"Yes. I want a relationship with you." His voice was quiet but firm, his hands sliding up my thighs. He looked at me as if he was completely in control of his emotions, utterly sure of the words coming out of his mouth. I yearned for that resolution, for that decision-making ability that he seemed to so cavalierly hold.

"I'm not available," I whispered. "Not fully. I *do* want a relationship with you. And it'd be exclusive ... except for him. If we dated, he would still be in my life. That's something you'd have to be okay with."

His face darkened, his hands tightening slightly on my skin. "You'd date both of us?"

I nodded silently, unable to look away from the train wreck that was occurring between our eyes. "I love him," I said simply.

I did.

I had fallen for Stewart quickly, despite the gaps of time that kept us apart, despite the little that I saw of him. He just... stayed with me. And it felt like every man I was with, every other touch I felt, was just a hollow substitute until I could have him again. Until Paul. Paul's touch, Paul's smile, had tugged at me in a new way. And I desperately hoped, as I straddled him in that rundown duplex, a siren sounding one street over, that he would understand. And... that he would agree.

He didn't agree. I could see the fight on his face, the inner turmoil pulling him this way or that. He sighed and sat up, our positions changing. Wrapping his arms around my waist, he pulled me tightly to him, crushing my breasts against the muscle of his chest, and planted a soft kiss on my neck. "I can't," he whispered. "I'm sorry, Madd."

It was the first time he called me that. I liked hearing it on his lips, even if it was attached to such a horrid decision. I left his place fifteen minutes later, wanting, hoping, he would say the nickname again so I could hear it roll off his tongue one last time. But he didn't. He only hugged me close, kissed the top of my head, and studied my eyes, as if he could find out some secret answer in their depths.

One week later, he showed up at the bookstore, his face flushed, eyes intense, and told me that he changed his mind.

"I don't like it," he muttered, running a hand through his hair, biting his bottom lip with a look of raw need that had me gripping the paperback in my hand a little tighter. "But ... I haven't been able to stop thinking about you. If it's what you want ... what you need, I'll give it a try."

We celebrated our new union right then and there. I pushed books aside and locked the doors, and he lowered me to the floor, his mouth frantic, ownership in every touch of his hands.

I think he was surprised at how easy it turned out to be. Our lives took on a seamless union, thanks to the separation of my two worlds. They don't meet. They don't talk. They don't ask questions about each other.

The separation was, and still is, the key that keeps this whole production running.

Now, I lie face down on his back. His muscles working smoothly underneath me as he paddles farther and farther from shore, the sounds of the city disappearing, replaced with seagulls and ocean surf. The waves subside and he rests. I close my eyes, enjoying the smooth rock of the board, the blanket of silence. A perfect, peaceful moment.

"I love you." His words are quiet.

I know. My unspoken thought floats away from our bodies. "I love you, too."

15

HOLLYWOOD, CA

My men are so different, yet similar in so many ways.

Their eyes. A similar tint of blue, but Paul's smile at me with carefree abandonment and Stewart's pierce my heart with their dark intensity.

Their bodies. Paul's is naturally muscular, his arms developed from hours of surfboard paddling, his abs ripped from balancing on a board, his thighs and calves strong from jumping, balancing, and kicking through currents. Stewart's body is attacked like everything else in his life, with fierce devotion, his aggression worked out with miles on a treadmill, weight-lifting, sit-ups, pull-ups, and calisthenics.

Their love. Paul loves me with unconditional warmth, his affection public and obvious, frequent and often. Stewart loves me with a tiger's intensity, one that takes my breath away, his confidence in our relationship strong enough to not be bothered by the presence of another man. He stares into my soul as if he owns it, and shows his love with money, sex, and rare moments of time.

Tonight is one of those rare moments. I have Stewart's full attention, his cell phone is away, and he is staring at me as if I contain everything needed to make his world whole. I step toward him, my new dress hugging my form to perfection. He sits up in the dining room chair, spreading his knees and patting his thigh, indicating where he wants me. I sit sideways on it, holding his gaze, and his hand steals up and runs lightly along my bare back. "You are breathtaking." His voice gruff, he leans forward and places a light kiss on my neck. "And you smell incredible."

"Thank you. You clean up pretty well yourself." And he does. In a tux that costs more than my dress, he looks every bit the successful executive he is. Short, orderly hair. Clean-shaven. Those intense eyes staring out of a strong face. "Is the car here?"

"It's downstairs. But it can wait." He runs a hand up my knee, sliding the material of the Versace cocktail dress up.

My breath shortens, my concentration focused on the path of his fingers as they travel higher, taking their time, the tickle of rough skin against soft flesh. He leans over, brushing a quick kiss over my lips and then moves lower, his kisses making the path down the line of my jaw, whispering across my neck, and deepening when they reach my collarbone. His hand caresses my thigh, the brush of his thumb moving higher until it is just breaths from my sex. I groan, sliding my hips forward, but his hand grips my thigh and holds me still. "Not yet. Let me enjoy you for a moment."

There is the sound of approaching footsteps, and I open my eyes to see our driver round the corner and stop short when we come into view. His eyes drop respectfully, and he speaks softly. "Mr. Brand, I'll be downstairs with the car when you are ready."

Stewart mutters something unintelligible, and the man takes the cue and leaves, pulling the door firmly closed behind him. Stewart pushes apart my legs, moving the fabric aside and leaving me bare and open to his eyes. He looks down, examining the exposed lips, and his mouth curves into a smile. "No panties?" His gaze flicks up to mine.

"They're in my purse. I figured they would be useless until we got to the event."

"That," he says softly, his fingers teasing the edge of my lips, circling the side of my pussy in slow, tantalizing brushes, each touch closer but not yet *there*, "is why I love you. You know me so well."

He stares at me, his eyes twin pools of lust and want. While Paul and I talk, incessantly, often, about anything and everything, important or not, Stewart and I fuck our way through this relationship, our time often too short for anything more than physical contact. Sex is how we connect—where we share our feelings, emotions, and love. I stare back at him, my eyes closing slightly when he rolls one confident finger over the knot of my clit, then down and into me, the small invasion a tease of perfection. "Look at me," he breathes. "I want to see your eyes."

I obey, my mouth parting as he cups my sex, slipping a second finger in with the first, both of them working together, stimulating me in their movement, his thumb staying firm on my clit, giving me soft pressure that moves slightly with each stroke of his fingers. He watches me, sees the moment that the fire of my need hits my eyes, sees the crescendo and burn of my arousal and adjusts the pace and pressure of his fingers in accordance with my want. The curl of pleasure grows, our eyes caught in a web of want, pulled to each other, and I barely notice the sexy pull of his mouth into a smile as my breathing increases, and I thrust into his action. His free hand slides up my chest and pulls on the fabric there, tugging my neckline down until a breast is exposed. He grips and tugs on it just hard enough to make me gasp.

"I want you like this forever," he whispers. "Spread open on my lap, shuddering in my hands, your pussy hot and tight around my fingers. You are so fucking beautiful."

I buck under his touch, my heels finding the floor and pushing off, my hand sliding up his pant leg, desperate to feel the heat of him in my hand before I come.

Blackness.

My eyes shut, and I moan, my legs convulsing around his fingers, the strum of his thumb on my clit softening, whisper soft, stretching out my pleasure as I cry out, over and over again. When it fades, when it softly pulls delicious heat from every area of my body, the need grows. Intense, animalistic desire, a craving for every bit of him in every place on my body. My eyes snap open and find him watching, a knowing grin already in place across that sexy mouth, his hand on his open fly, pulling out the object of my desire and stroking its hard length against my bare leg.

I push his back against the chair and step over him, straddling his waist and lowering myself down, so wet I drip, my need so great that I moan. He catches my weight, carrying my ass down and impaling me with his cock, his own groan sounding in the large room, his eyes darkening as I tighten around him. "God, you were made for me."

"I'm your dirty little slut," I whisper, sliding up and down, my heels firm on the floor, his hands tilting and pulling my ass how he likes it, in a way that causes my clit to rub against his pelvis, the tight squeeze on my ass pleasurable in its slight bit of pain.

"You *are* my slut," he grounds out. "You need my cock."

"So badly," I agree. "I can't get enough of it."

He thrusts from below, pulling me down, the extra depth causing me to gasp, my body to grind, the pleasure shooting a spike of arousal through my core. "Tell me you love me."

"I love you."

"Again." He thrusts, sitting up, looking into my eyes, our faces inches apart as I look slightly down on him.

"I love you," I whisper, gripping the back of his chair.

Then his eyes close, and he leans back, tugging the other side of my dress down, exposing both breasts to his hands. And I know what he wants. I know, just like I know every inch of his body, exactly what he needs. I lean back, my hands resting on his knees, my back arched, my body open before him, and fuck his cock. Pumping up and down on his so-hard-it-will-break shaft, my legs supporting my body, his gaze skimming greedily along my skin, his hand lifting the hem of my dress, fingers strumming the bead of my clit until I come—body tightening, mouth screaming, world exploding.

Then he takes over, leaning forward and scooping me into and against his chest. My legs wrap tightly around his body, his cock stiff and slick inside my body, he carries me over to the wall, presses me up against it, and holds me there with strong arms. Then, he thrusts over and over again, whispering my name softly, and then louder, until he comes with a massive groan, his legs shaking beneath him, my own wobbly when he lowers me to my feet. He keeps me there, pinning me against the wall with his body, my breasts tight against his tuxedo, his hands stealing into my hair, his mouth soft and sweet on mine. Drinking from my mouth, tasting me, taking his time, inhaling my scent.

"I missed you this week. I needed that." His voice is gravelly, thick with satisfaction and truth. He tilts my head up, looks into my eyes, then lowers his mouth back to mine.

16

HOLLYWOOD, CA

A-FRAME: [NOUN]

**LARGE WAVE WITH DISTINCT SHOULDERS ON THE LEFT
AND RIGHT SIDE OF THE PEAK. CAN RESULT IN TWO
SURFERS SURFING THE SAME WAVE . . . ONE GOING
FRONTSIDE AND THE OTHER GOING BACKSIDE.**

Two hours later, my fingers steal under the tablecloth. Reaching over and gripping Stewart's leg, my fingers deftly slide up his thigh, his hand catching mine, eyes shooting a questioning look in my direction.

He coughs gently, breaking eye contact as he glances to the woman on his right. "That's correct, Beth. With quarterly projections where they're at, there should be no need for additional debt. If anything, we should capitalize on our current assets." He listens to her response, his hand firm on mine, keeping me at bay.

But I *need* him. I need to feel his strength beneath my hand, to feel his arousal in my grip. When the conversation changes course, he leans over, planting a soft kiss on my neck and whispers in my ear. "Do you need something?"

"Yes. You. Now." It is an unfair request, one I shouldn't make, but I am panting for him. I will not make it through this four-hour dinner, through the polite chitchat that will follow, cigars in the men's club while I sit with dignified wives in the front parlor. I need a release, need firm hands digging into my skin, his mouth on mine, cock inside of me.

He studies me, a war going on behind those eyes, his glance flitting around the table and then down at his watch. He leans forward again, close enough that I can smell his scent, the masculinity crawling across the table and robbing me of rational thought. He grips my wrist, pulling my hand tightly and places it on his crotch, brushing his lips against my ear as he speaks. "Call him."

I pull back, confused, but his hand cups the back of my head, keeping me close to him. I study the tumultuous depths of his blue eyes. "What? Who?"

"*Him*. Call him. Have him take care of you. I can't leave."

There is only one *Him* in our life, our world comprised of three people. I try to process his words, spoken without anger or light, in a serious, I'm-not-fucking-around tone. I shake my head, and his eyes sharpen at my reaction, his hand pushing mine down on his cock. His voice rasps in my ear, thick with arousal and authority. "I want it, Madison. I want him to fuck you in the powder room while I sit here with these stuffed shirts. I want you to come back to this table with your cheeks flushed and his cum inside of you."

I feel the twitch of him beneath my hand, see the flicker of excitement in his eyes, and realize the truth of his words. "Seriously?" I whisper, almost afraid to voice the question.

He slides my hand over him, letting me feel the hard ridge of his arousal. It is pushing at his pants, his excitement unquestionably hard. "Call him. Now."

I sit there for a moment, the hum of conversation muting as my mind processes this new avenue. My need moans between my legs, its intensity doubled by Stewart's words, by the twitch of him that proved his sincerity. *Can I go there?* Can I bring these two worlds so close and still escape with our dual relationships intact?

It only takes a moment to make the decision.

I excuse myself and step away, pulling out my phone, watching the dark gleam in Stewart's eyes, a sexy smile crossing his lips. He's serious. He wants me to be fucked while he sits a few rooms away, surrounded by wealth and business. I dial Paul's number, biting my lower lip and move farther away from the table, holding Stewart's gaze.

"Hey babe." Paul's voice is lazy, as if he'd dozed off on the couch.

"Come to Hollywood. The W Hotel. I need your cock."

A minute later, I return to the table and smile demurely at Stewart, who rises at my entrance and pulls out my chair, his napkin hiding any erection he may have. Leaning down as he pushes my chair in, he softly speaks. "Is he coming?"

"There are so many places I could go with that question," I murmur. "But yes."

He sits back down, reaching for his wine glass and smiling at me. "Good."

I try to pay attention to the conversation. Try to eat my salad and smile politely, nod appropriately, laugh when the overweight man to my right makes a joke. But I am waiting, my leg jiggling nervously. Waiting for the buzz of my phone against my leg, for the moment he is here.

My call had surprised him, his voice hardening when he heard my directive. I could imagine him sitting up, trying to put the pieces together, hearing the raw need in my voice. He knows me as well as Stewart does. He knows that when my blood rushes and need hits me, there is only one thing that can satisfy it. Cock. Thrust roughly, taking my body as its own. He knows I can't contain it, that the need grows and expands until my fingers or someone else's body fucks it to sleep. He knows I won't want to make love. He knows I'll need my brains fucked out, and he knows exactly how I like that done. As Stewart does. They have memorized my body, learned my tells, and fucked me enough that every movement is delivered before I have to ask.

I am brought back to the present when I hear Stewart speak, his expression calm and intelligent, the rough scrape of his voice only audible to me, who knows it so well. I can see the slight tightening of his jaw, can see the fire in his eyes when he casually glances my way. He is aroused and allows my hand to confirm it when I reach over. Full-blown, hard as a diamond, aroused. It confuses the hell out of me and makes me wet at the same time. Then my phone buzzes, and I am out of time to think.

I stand, gripping my purse, waving the men off as they start to rise. "I'm sorry, I'm not feeling well. I'm going to step outside for a bit."

False concern crosses Stewart's features as he rises, excusing himself and escorting me to the door. "You will be the death of me, you know that?" he says softly.

"I could say the same for you."

He stops just before the door. "Have him fuck you hard," he bites out, pulling me into his body with sudden aggression. "And whatever he doesn't take care of, I will. Just give me a few hours to finish up this business. But hurry." He gives my ass a possessive squeeze, hard enough to sting, my panties soaked at the forbidden nature of this entire experience. I grip my purse tightly and step out of the restaurant, into the hotel lobby and head for the restroom.

I knock gently on the unisex door. "It's me." My voice croaks on the last word. This is the closest my two worlds have ever come to colliding. Stewart and Paul, in the same building. My dark and my light. My dark now seated, surrounded by finery, listening attentively to talks of profit and loss, his cock hard, hidden underneath fine linens and discussions of intellect. And my light, swinging the door open and pulling me inside, slamming it closed behind me and flipping the latch. No words were spoken as he thrust me against the door, his mouth greedy on mine as he tastes champagne on my tongue, our need thick in the air. I reach for him, my hand running down his worn tee and grip the top of his jeans. He has not changed clothes since I saw him last, has not dressed up for his entrance into this hotel, and I love the contrast. His messy hair to Stewart's combed. Five o'clock shadow to clean-shaven. The smell of sweat to cologne. I normally get a cleansing period, the twenty-minute drive between my worlds clearing my head, my skin, my palette. Now, walking instantly from one to the other, the comparisons are overwhelming. He pulls back, releasing me. Wiping a hand over his mouth, his eyes take a slow tour of my body.

"Look at you," he whispers. "Dressed up like you are a good girl." He hasn't seen me like this. With my hair conservative and a cocktail dress on, pearls at my neck. He slides my dress up, the expensive fabric stiff, a black triangle of lace panties exposed. I stay still, my back against the wall, legs slightly forward and spread a few feet apart. My chest heaves, need gripping me, and I watch him unzip his pants and pull out his cock.

"Suck it. On your knees in this bathroom. Suck my cock while your boyfriend sits at the table."

There is an edge to his voice, an anger that is not normally present. An emotion that turns my easy-going Paul into something darker. *Sexier*. I love it, love the bite in his voice, the possession in his hand as he grips the back of my head and pulls me fully onto his cock. He thrusts into my mouth, his eyes on mine, the connection between us unbroken as he fucks my throat, growing harder with every pump, the fire in his eyes making the need between my legs almost painful in its intensity.

I pull off him and gasp for breath, then he's pulling me to my feet before I can even speak, pinning me to his body as his hand wraps around and slides underneath the edge of my dress and squeezes my ass. *Hard.* So hard I gasp, his eyes tight on mine and he releases it, running his fingers down the crack of my ass and fingering the channel of my sex, covered in lace. His fingers run back and forth over the spot, a grin stretching across his face at the dampness there.

"Is that for me or him?"

I don't answer, reaching between our bodies and fisting his cock. I wrap my hand tightly around it, every vein in the organ outlined in the rigidity of his arousal.

"Answer me, Madd. Answer me while I fuck you right here. While I make you scream so loud that people walking by will hear."

"Make me," I whisper, a challenge in my tone.

His grip around my waist tightens, his eyes holding mine with a fierce look as he listens to my words.

"Make me scream your name while he conducts his business. Make me your slut, right here and now, and send me back to him with your cum dripping out of me."

He groans and pushes me back against the wall, spreading my legs with his knees. He reaches down with both hands, grips my panties and yanks, ripping the sheer fabric with one strong jerk. Then he's back against me, his hard chest against mine, his bare cock rough and bobbing at my entrance, pushing for and then finding the wetness and pushing inside. "Jesus Christ, Madd," he groans, shoving upward, his hard thighs pinning me to the wall, his hands yanking at my straps, pulling my cashmere cardigan off my shoulders and jerking the top of my dress down. He thrusts again, his thighs relaxing and then flexing, every fuck bouncing me back against the wall, his hands clasping my breasts, squeezing them into his palms.

"Make me scream," I grit out, my eyes on his. They are tortured blue, cloudy with arousal, latent with need. "You know that he fucked me? Before we came here. I straddled his cock and rode him. His hands were rough on me, his cock taking my body. He was bare inside me, Paul, right where you are now." He roars, his voice raw and primal, holding me against the wall, losing control as he slams into me, faster and faster, until my body becomes a shaking sea of desire, my core rattled, gasping, his thrusts urgent and dominant, his breath ragged, his hands finding my face and bringing my mouth to his.

"You are mine," he grunts out, pumping into me, the length and level of his arousal brutal.

"Mine," he swears, as he releases my mouth and turns me around, pushing me forward as he yanks my hips back, one hand hard on my back, the other gripping my ass. He doesn't slow the movement, giving me full, hard thrusts, my cleavage bouncing out of the top of my dress, the mirror above the sink giving me a full view of my slutdom.

Paul, his hair mussed, mouth open, intensity over his face. His reflection pulls at my hair, tilting my head back, and I find his eyes on mine in the mirror.

"You like what you see?" His words are terse, thick. He is conflicted, but—from the level of his erection—fully aroused, his speed increasing, his breathing loud in the small space. "You like being fucked while he's in the next room?"

I don't answer, my climax too close, every muscle in my body tightening in anticipation of the act, throbbing and contracting around him, his eyes closing briefly at the sensation.

"God, Madd. You are so fucking good ..." He pulls out abruptly, leaving me gasping, my chest aching as I turn to him, feeling his hands before I fully move; they shove me back, wrapping around my waist and lifting me, setting me on the low counter of the sink, and pulling me to the edge. He jacks himself, looking at my pussy, at the swollen pink lips of my sex, then glances up to meet my eyes. He steps forward, pressing himself against my opening, pulling up my chin when he sees me glance down. "Look at me. Look at me and tell me what he did to you. Tell me what he did, and make me come all fucking up inside of you."

I close my eyes at his first thrust, the angle different, better, brushing along my g-spot. "He sat me on his lap, in this same dress. Those panties? The ones you ripped to shreds? I wasn't wearing those when I first saw him. Because I knew he'd take me as soon as he could."

He pulls halfway out, and the view of his dick, slick with me, is the hottest thing I've ever seen. His hands tighten and he pushes deep, dragging his cock in and out of me in long, full strokes. My voice catches at the look in his eyes, the intensity of his arousal. All playfulness is gone. This man before me—he is Stewart, but with different features, their similarities never more present than right now, and I gasp when he completely buries himself inside.

"More," he groans. "Tell me more."

"I came from his fingers, my juices all over his hand. I came and I screamed his name when I did it. I told him how fucking perfect he was and how much he turned me on." His strokes roughened with my words, increasing in speed, his competitiveness lighting a fire in my belly, and I was suddenly *there* again. On the brink of orgasm, need running through my limbs and pumping loud in my heart. "God, Paul, you have no idea how good his cock feels in me. How deep he goes when I straddle him and fuck him hard. How he whispers my name when I take every inch of him."

He roars, pulling me to the far edge of the sink, thrusting deeper and harder than he ever has, his mouth roughly taking my own, his tongue marking, branding, and drinking from my mouth. I push against his chest, my body breaking in his arms, the orgasm whirling through me, my words tumbling out as I shudder with pleasure in his arms, his pace never slowing, his cries joining my own, the hot spread of liquid pumped deep with his cock, his name repeated over and over as he finally, with one final shuddering thrust, empties himself inside me.

Five minutes later, I slip back into my seat, Stewart barely pausing in a lengthy explanation of market trends and their expected impact. But I feel his attention on me, see the casual glance at his watch. "Impressive," he murmurs, tugging my hand to his lips and placing a soft kiss on my knuckles. "I take it you are taken care of?"

I feel drugged, heady with the release and the knowledge of what I have just done. "Until tonight," I whisper.

"Oh, have no doubt," he says, staring into my eyes. "You will need every bit of energy you have for it."

I hide a grin behind a long sip of champagne, turning when I feel a soft hand on my arm.

"My wife tells me you sell books," the man says, a polite smile on his face. "Tell me, what authors do you enjoy?"

I smile politely, responding to the man, and feel the rough heat of Stewart's hand, sliding up my dress, and hear his intake of breath when he finds my lack of panties.

We leave the event early. Stewart declines invitations for cigars and blames my lightheadedness for our early departure. He pulls me by the hand, his steps clipped, my heels skittering to keep up. We push through the lobby doors and into the cool night air, the valet ready with his car, the intense look on his face as he shuts my door sending shivers through my body.

The engine roars as he accelerates out of the garage, his hand fumbling for and unbuckling my seatbelt as he turns onto the road, the traffic light. "I need your fucking mouth on me. Now." He loosely grips my hair and pulls as I bend over the center console and quickly undo his belt, his erection strong against the expensive fabric of his slacks.

He grunts when I have it out, my hand gripping it, my mouth on it before he can speak, precum salty and sweet on my tongue, proof of his arousal. His hand pushes my head down, and he exhales as I take him. "Jesus, Madison." His voice breaks, almost as if on a cry, the need so strong, his grip shaking as he cups the back of my head. "I couldn't fucking think in there. Knowing what you were doing, knowing what you had done. My sweet, fucking girl, full of another man." He thrusts upward on the final word, his sentence ending harshly, thick with competition.

I suck, hard and fast, my hand aiding me, the push and pull of his hand setting the tone, my mouth doing the rest. And it doesn't take long. He is so ready, so primed for me, three hours of buildup turning my steel man into a mess of want and desire. It is gorgeous when he comes.

Gasping my name...

thrusting into my mouth...

twitching, spurting, more and more...

draining down my throat, spilling out around my hand.

I gag, I gulp and he says my name, over and over, his thighs flexing beneath me, his grip tight on my hair.

His car flies into the portico of his building, and he slams on the brakes, shoving the car into park and groaning for air as both hands come down on my head, pushing himself up into my mouth for one last thrust, one final drop. Then he pulls me back, lifting under my arms and dragging me across the center, his arms encasing me as I curl into a ball against his hard chest. A chest that is heaving, his heart pounding beneath his tux, his arms wrapping tightly around my body.

"God..." he whispers. "You are my fucking kryptonite." He leans down, pressing soft kisses on my hair and forehead, his hand releasing me and cradling my face, turning it up to his, before kissing me fully and deeply on the lips. "I love you, Madison. For everything."

—

And that is how it is. I fuck Stewart, I fuck Paul, and they both know about it. And the more I fuck one, the more turned on the other gets. The more competitive, aggressive, loving they become. It is a constant, whirling sea of sex. I love it, and they love it. They don't need to know details about the other man. That would take it a step too close, a step too real. It is better that it is a faceless individual, and I appreciate keeping the worlds separate. I've had fantasies, sure. Thought about having them both at the same time, their hands on my body, their competing cocks battling over my skin. But that just seems too messy. And I don't want to do anything to disrupt the perfection that is us. The three of us. Living two separate relationships.

I get that you don't understand—that you wonder how someone could possibly be aroused by the thought of something so forbidden. But often, it is the forbidden that is the hottest, and the depraved that is the most arousing.

17

TORRANCE, CA

DANA

It is unhealthy, this obsession I have with Stewart's love life. Why should it matter who he dates? Why do I care if the blushing blonde on his arm is a flavor of the week or a future wife? I should return to my life and focus on decorating my empty condo and finishing my stacks of work. I shouldn't care whether he's happy or lonely, a workaholic or a loving boyfriend. But of course, I care. I will always care. I will always love him, and I will always watch out for him. He is my Stewart.

And the blonde from the bookstore—if she is a flavor of the week, she's stretched her flavor into months. Some may call it stalking, some might call it love, but I'm continuing to watch them from afar. I see her leave his building, flashing the valet a familiar smile as she catches the keys and slips into her expensive convertible. I've followed her onto the freeway, the woman driving recklessly, quickly losing me in traffic as I attempt to use a blinker, maintain a safe speed, and not nose dive beneath the tread of an eighteen-wheeler. She is gone, the white car whipping into the glare of the

California sun, headed east, my sleuthing attempt a disaster. At least I got her tag number, the five digits written in neat script on my notepad. Too bad I have no idea of what to do with it.

Maybe he's happy. I hope he is. I called him this afternoon. But again, as it's been for three years, he did not answer.

18

LUNADA BAY, CA

CRUSHER: [NOUN]

**SOMEONE WHO SURFS HARD, AS IF THEY HAVE NOTHING
TO LOSE AND NO FEAR INSIDE**

MADISON

Lunada Bay is Paul's favorite place to surf, waves high and
dangerous enough to heat his blood and put a smile on his face. It is
also one of the most contested spots to stick your board in. It's
located in Rancho Palos Verdes, which is pretty much where all rich
white people go to die. Colossal mansions sit oceanfront, with
manicured lawns and Mercedes that stare out onto waves that kill
at least one surfer a year. The local surfers are territorial, running
off tourists with sharp voices often backed up by fists, keeping the
waves uncluttered and the beach sunbather free. In the '90s, a local
television crew was attacked, broken bottles and punches causing
blood and bruised egos to scamper back up the slippery slope to
the road, their broadcasts interrupted by a trip to the ER.

But... they allow Paul. They are in awe of him, as am I—his effort-less conquer of the waves, his ability, no matter how rough or dangerous a spill, to resurface in the froth. But he wasn't always allowed. I've seen his scar, a long, thick knot of tissue where some spoiled rich kook slashed his side in an attempt to protect this jewel-encrusted strip of beach. Paul returned the next day and battled waves while bleeding through thirty-four stitches. After that, they accepted him as their own, and, when I came into his life, welcomed me with sunburnt smiles.

Today, the waves are almost twelve feet. Surfers measure from the back, so a twelve-foot wave is actually, from the shore, twenty-four feet in height, a huge wall of dark water, rising like a beast before curling and crashing onto any surfer foolish or unlucky enough to be in its grasp. I look for Paul, searching for his red board, not seeing his head bobbing among the riders. My arms tighten around my knees, my eyes scanning slowly, then quickly, and I try to recount the last time I saw him.

Then I see his board, my nerves replaced by a quick rush of relief. He is out farther, a few hundred yards behind the main peak, at a spot called Truck Drivers. My heart sinks, doom dragging it down until it sits somewhere in my stomach, heavy as lead, my breaths coming short and fast.

"Whoa, Paul's taking Truck Drivers?"

I don't turn at the voice, knowing its source. *Rayne*. A dreadlocked Barbie who rarely lifts her head off her boyfriend's cock or the bong he places before her. "Yeah."

"He is crazyyyy, girl."

He *is* crazy. Truck Drivers is a take-off spot for waves, named by some local who had probably died shortly after naming it. It's for daredevils, or anyone stupid enough to want to risk their life for a wave. And the wave that's coming? It's beautiful. Terrifyingly so.

"Uh-oh," Rayne says softly. I don't know whether to slap her or bury my face in her massive chest and avoid the entire thing.

But I can't move. I'm glued to the scene, glued to his form, as he leans forward, lying flat and low on the board and begins paddling, the wave growing larger and more deadly as it develops.

The ocean is a beast. A beast that doesn't care if it chews you up or swallows you whole. A beast you cannot beat—you can only dance with it until the time comes when it kills you. It will never lose, and with moves like this, Paul is living on borrowed time. I watch him paddle toward it and wonder if this is the moment when he will die.

The wall of water raises straight up, sunlight glinting off it in a way that hurts my eyes. I stand, my eyes locked on the one small break in its awesome silhouette, the dip that is my heart, the man I love standing on the board and disappearing into its churn as it breaks, bending down on itself, Paul's body gone, nothing but white energy before me.

Right now, he's in one of two places. In the channel, hidden by the wave of water, or he's fallen, crushed underwater by the wave.

A breaking wave can push a surfer down twenty to fifty feet, sending them into a washing-machine style spin that tumbles and breaks them apart. When they finally stop spinning, when their chest is breaking apart and fighting against the urge to inhale, they have to regain equilibrium and figure out which way is up. Some surfers swim the wrong way, traveling ten feet before their bursting lungs and their sense of direction alerts them to the deadly mistake. Lack of air isn't the only danger. Water pressure at that depth will rupture an eardrum as easily as crushing a fly. Even worse is not having any depth. If the ocean floor or a reef is present, the wave will grind you against it like a mortar to a stone. Paul *needs* to get to the surface before the next wave hits. The next wave will be a new downward force, a second round in the spin cycle. A second round that will compound the danger, one that his lungs will probably not survive.

A flash of red. Breaking waves. Far left, shooting out of the front of the curl, Paul's board dipping down and ahead of the break, swinging up, and then down again, his body stepping forward on the nose, arms loose and confident, his movement graceful and relaxed.

I gasp. For him, it was nothing. For me, I just died a small death. I blink back tears and sink to the sand.

"Chocka," Rayne drawls, brushing off her arms and stepping away.

19

HOLLYWOOD, CA

Paul left this afternoon for San Diego, where a tropical storm has created a current he wants to chase. He kissed me quickly, throwing some clothes in a bag and promised to be back tomorrow afternoon unless the weather changes. I am used to it, his excitement over perfect conditions, the unending quest for the perfect wave. It will be a personal victory, a conquer that no one will see, and there's some nobility in that.

I watch him leave, then dial Stewart's cell. He doesn't answer, and my texts go unreturned. I mill around the house for a bit, then grab my keys and head into Hollywood.

I valet my car and take the elevator up, inserting my key and pressing the button for his suite. At eight pm, the chances are that he's still at work. But I can wait, change into comfortable clothes and grab something from the fridge.

Entering the suite, I hear his voice and follow it down the hall and into his office.

He is on the phone, his face tired, small lines outlining his handsome features. He looks up, surprised, and a smile stretched over his face. He turns in his chair, away from his desk, and taps his thigh, pulling me into his chest when I sit.

I stay there for a while, his hand rubbing along my back as he listens, the motion stopping when he speaks, his other hand scribbling figures on a pad of paper. I can hear the voice in his ear, the phone stuck in the crook of his shoulder, a fast-paced dialogue about product placement, market awareness, and sales trends.

I bore quickly and slide off his lap, into the opening between his legs, my hand running over his belt, my gaze moving up to catch his. He watches me wordlessly, his eyes urging me to continue, the push of bone under my wrist letting me know he is ready.

He's always ready. His cock seems engineered to spring into action at a moment's notice. It is one of the things I love about him. I unbuckle his pants and stand, pulling my sundress over my head slowly, letting him see every inch of what he will soon get.

20

STEWART

She is beautiful. I knew that from the moment I first saw her, through snow flurries, a grin on her face like she captured the world and just threw it back. But I didn't really know how beautiful she was until I knew her. Until I saw into her soul and became lost in her goodness. The final step of my capture came when she lost her clothes. Bared her body—that body I see in my dreams, jack off to in the morning, and worship in her presence. And now, with her pulling every inch of that yellow sundress up and off her curves ... I'm lost. I am lost, and she has found me. I hang up the phone mid-sentence and unplug the cord from its back.

I roll my chair forward, running my hands along the back of her legs, traveling up the curves of her ass, gripping the skin there as I lean forward and kiss her, tasting the hint of salt that tells me she has been in the ocean. I slide my fingers under the cloth of her underwear, simple pink boy-shorts that I tug down, over the tan curves of her hips, the faint strips of pale tan lines. Then the under-wear hits the floor, and she is bare before me. I start to stand, but she pushes me down, pins me to the chair as she kneels, a playful smile on her face, a gleam of fire in her eyes.

I love her eyes. Love how I can instantly tell if she is mad, excited, or in love. Whatever the emotion, whatever her temperature that day, there is always sex in those eyes. It floats off her skin, gleams in her eyes, and is in every move of her delicious body. This woman cannot exist without sex. It is her food, her body-sustaining air. I discovered that early, knew it from our second date. She cannot contain it, and doesn't even try. She embraces it, owns it, loves it. She does not fuck out of insecurity or to get something or someone. She fucks because she loves it and loves through it. It is her gift to the world, and I am lucky enough to be a part of that world.

She feels the strength of my arousal, her smile brilliant in my dim office. Then she unzips me, and I am in her mouth.

Fuckkkk. I will never be able to accurately describe her mouth. It is like a throbbing pulse of wet, hot moisture, seconded only by her body. It knows how hard to suck, how deep to go, how fast or slow to take my cock, and when to give it a moment to regroup. Her eyes flicker to mine, heat in their gaze, and I want nothing more than to pull her to her feet and bend her over my desk. I place my hand at the back of her head, watching in drugged awe as my length slides deeper into her mouth, her pink lips tight around me, the playful gleam in her eyes making my cock harden even further.

I pull back on her hair, trying to lift her up, but she shakes her head, burying me greater, her eyes closing as she gags on my cock. She grips me tightly with her hand, sliding it up and down my shaft, squeezing it, and I feel every bit of stress in my body leave, as if she is milking it out of me. I sigh and lean back in my chair, content to let her work.

She's beautiful when she sucks a cock. Her cheeks hollow, her mouth curves when she pulls off, her mischievousness telegraphs how much she truly enjoys the act.

I groan, feeling the pressure of buildup. I'm throbbing in her mouth, close to climax, the three days without her taking their toll on my self-control.

"Fuck baby." I lean forward and cup the back of her neck, intently watching the movement in and out of her mouth. "Here I come."

She takes me fully, her mouth massaging and squeezing the length of me, my head deep in her throat when I come. Wave after wave of release, my hand unintentionally tightening on her neck, my pleasure audible and uncontainable.

She swallows it all. When she finally pulls off me—my dick clean—a smile stretches across her face.

I collapse back in my seat, tugging her gently into my arms, her body curling onto my lap. "Thank you, baby. I needed that." I rest my head on hers. "I'm surprised you're here. Thought I wouldn't see you until this weekend."

"He had to run down to San Diego. I thought I'd stop by, give you some loving and stay the night. Maybe kidnap you into a breakfast date."

I frown against her hair. "Can't do breakfast. I have a six AM call with Helsinki."

She tilts her head up, brushes her lips across the rough shadow on my neck. "Then how about I cook you breakfast at five?"

I wrap my arms around her, including her arms and legs in the grip. "That would be perfect. Need me to take care of you?"

She bites my neck lightly. "No. Get back to your work. I'll wake you at five." She pushes at my arms, breaking free of my grip and standing, her naked skin glowing in the light from the lamp. I pull her back, getting one last taste of her mouth, before plugging my phone back in and returning to the documents on my desk. As she leaves, tugging the door shut behind her, the phone rings.

21

ACID DROP: [VERB]

**WHEN YOU TAKE OFF ON A WAVE AND SUDDENLY HAVE
THE BOTTOM FALL OUT AND FREE FALL DOWN THE FACE.**

DANA

It's Wednesday night, and I'm in PJs and socks, a face mask beginning to dry on my face, as I sit in front of the television, popcorn in
the microwave. Cross-legged, my back against the edge of my way-
too-expensive-but-I-love-it couch, I'm flipping through channels
and trying to resist the urge to touch my face and see if the mask
has hardened.

Soap opera. Flip.

Infomercial. Flip.

Football. Flip.

Surfing.

I pause, my remote extended, waiting to see what the show is about, which hotspot or event is being covered. And then I see Paul, trudging through sand, a board tucked under his arm, that one-in-a-million smile lighting his tan face. My breath catches as I see pure, effortless happiness, no sign of the haunted Paul I remember. Then, there is a blur of blonde, a streak before the camera, a bundle of bikini and cover-up throwing herself into his arms, gripping his neck, and placing a kiss on his cheek. A girl. Maybe she's the reason for his happiness, for the light that shines from his eyes. Or maybe she is a groupie, one of the hundreds of beach Barbies that follow the surfing circuit. I listen to the announcer's recount of Paul, of his awards and standings, watching as he swings the girl in a tight circle before setting her down. He pulls her in for a full kiss before she bashfully pushes him away. She turns, and I see her face.

It hurts, the expression I make, the contortion of my face as my jaw drops and eyes open wide, dried edges of the mask pulling and protesting as I stare in shock.

Her.

Tucked under Stewart's arm, their faces beaming as they walked past me in Livello.

A carefree wave to the valet as she left Stewart's world and headed elsewhere.

On her knees, surrounded by books, spewing out friendliness as she gave away lighthearted mysteries.

Her. Stewart's love, the reason for his smile. Hugging Paul. Kissing Paul.

The camera flips to another surfer, and my world blurs, my thoughts moving too quickly for rational thought, question after question pounding through my mind. In the background, the microwave shrills, a persistent beep, shrieking and shrieking, like the countdown timer to a bomb of horrific proportions.

What. The. *Fuck.* Is. Going. On?

22

HOLLYWOOD, CA

MADISON

I enter our bedroom, flipping on the lights and heading for the shower, a huge space with twelve body jets and a rain head that could accommodate The Hulk. Twenty minutes later, I crawl into bed and turn on the television. Halfway through a stain-remover infomercial, I fall asleep.

At some point in the night, Stewart joins me, pulling me tight to his body, his mouth soft against the back of my neck. I nestle into his chest, murmuring his name, and sleep steals back over me. The next thing I hear is the soft ding of my alarm.

I move, half-awake, through the motions of cooking. Preheating a skillet. Pouring oil. Beating eggs. The bacon is sizzling in the pan when I lick my fingers and move down the hall, pressing the button that opens the blinds. They move, a soft hum of motors, light peeking through the large windows, the bedroom still dim, dawn on the edge of our city's horizon.

"Wakey, wakey," I sing, running my hands lightly through Stewart's hair before planting a soft kiss on his lips. They move beneath my mouth, smiling, and he speaks against my kiss, his eyes still closed.

"It can't be five already."

"It is, baby. I don't joke about interrupting sleep. I've got bacon in the pan, so I've got to get back to the stove." I steal another kiss and then leave, trailing my hands across his bare chest, then jog back to the kitchen, snagging a pair of tongs and turning over crispy bacon a moment before it burns.

I have the bacon on a plate and am scooping eggs out when I feel him enter, his heavy presence as palatable as a burst of hot air. I grin, knowing what is coming even before I feel his hands on my ass, gripping and squeezing before sliding his hands around my stomach, coming up and brushing my breasts. He nuzzles my neck. "You can't possibly expect me to eat food when you're naked."

"I'm not naked. I'm *almost* naked," I protest, slipping out of his hands and carrying our plates to the bar. "Now sit. I didn't get up at 4:30 to have you ignore my breakfast."

He obeys, moving my plate until it is next to his and pats the stool. "Well, almost naked, if that is what you call it, looks damn tempting."

"Thank you." I gestured to the sheer teddy. "You can thank Valentine's Day last year for that."

He tilts his head. "Is that what I got you?"

"And a watch. But I didn't feel like dripping diamonds while flipping bacon."

He grins. "Understandable."

"What's the call with Helsinki about?"

"Rebranding. We're splitting an entity into two parts and need a new brand for the new arm."

Stewart works for a venture capitalist firm. They purchase assets that are struggling, then paint a new face on them, streamline their production processes, and use their bulk buying power and outsourcing to reduce costs. Many of his subcontractors are in Finland and India, which makes every hour of the day a business hour. He treats his new assets like children, becoming emotionally invested in their futures, their successes, and their failures. I love his passion and understand the time commitment and place in his life that his work possesses. In his life, work is first, and I'm second. I am okay with that standing, just as he's okay with the fact that I will not make our relationship exclusive as long as I have that second-place ranking.

It doesn't stop me from loving him any less. It doesn't stop my heart from tugging when he smiles. It doesn't stop my recognition that he loves me back, as much as his heart and schedule will allow. I don't want our world to be any different than it is right now. A change in his priorities would mean a change in our relationship. A change in our relationship would mean that I'd have to choose between him and Paul. And I can't do that. Not right now. I'm not ready for that jump.

He glances at the kitchen clock and leans over, placing a soft kiss on the edge of my lips. "Leave the dishes, babe. Estelle will be here soon. I'm going to take that call."

I nod. "Sounds good. I'm gonna head back to bed."

And I do. I lose the teddy and matching thong and crawl into bed, the motorized blinds dragging the room back into darkness. My heavy breakfast and early morning causes sleep to come quickly, and I don't wake until almost eleven.

23

VENICE BEACH, CA

The bookstore is busy, a rare occurrence, and the afternoon passes quickly. I sell a grand total of sixty used books, bringing in a whopping hundred bucks. The new books have a nice showing also, bringing the owner some much-needed revenue and guaranteeing me at least one more month of employment. I lock up at eight and head next door to the bar that shares our awning.

It's crowded, a mix of tourists and locals, familiar smiles flashing as I grab a bar stool. Bip, a pretty brunette that has managed to look eighteen for a good ten years longer than physically possible, pops a Corona open and slides it over to me.

"Thanks."

"No sweat, babe. Where's your sexier half?"

"Somewhere on I-5. He's with Nick and Moses, headed back from Del Mar."

"They catch good conditions?"

"According to the text I got, the waves were great, but too many shoobies, so it was a zoo."

"That's the problem with this time of year. Tourists everywhere." She lowered her voice, glancing around before shooting me a smile. "Not that I'm complaining."

"Hey, me either." I toasted her, taking a swig of the beer and glancing at my watch. "Can you put in a large Philly to go? I'm gonna head home before it gets too crazy."

Venice Beach has been romanticized by Hollywood and an impressively deceptive tourism marketing campaign. They paint our sidewalk stands and street performers in a romantic light, touting our artistic graffiti and muscle beach as unique oddities. In actuality, it's the armpit of LA tourism. Panhandlers and druggies everywhere, homeless getting rich off intimidated tourists and families that are too far from the safety of their car to say no. We have at least ten murders a year, over three hundred aggravated assaults, and around a hundred rapes. The majority of those crimes happen to tourists, prostitutes, and drug users. Paul and I fall in the lower-risk demographic, but that doesn't mean we are safe. Locals do their best to protect other locals, our misfit band of eccentrics attempting some basic form of civility. But I am a young, attractive female. Walking down the boardwalk after dark alone scares me. I call Paul and let him know I'm on my way home.

"Awesome, babe. I'm twenty minutes away. Gonna drop the boys at their place, and then I'll be home. Call me when you get to the house, so I know you're safe."

I agree, hanging up my cell and slip it into the pocket of my sweatshirt. Then I grab my food, throw a twenty on the bar, and head into the crowded night, a half-mile from home.

I move quickly through the crowds, my hood up despite the warm night air, ignoring the catcalls from men and panhandlers who know me yet still stick out their hands. I nod to familiar faces and share words with a few locals. Then, the crowds thin, and I am on the sparse path that covers the last quarter-mile home. There are still tourists here, ones who didn't realize that the South Venice parking lot was the wrong place to park, a long walk from the attractions, a much closer lot a quarter-mile north. We all hurry, the night sky unsettling, too many shadows and dark alleys in between the million-dollar bungalows that face this oceanfront, broken sidewalk.

I reach our street, head a block east and jog up the steps to our home, my key out and ready, the deadbolt flipping in the lock as soon as the door is shut. I strip off my sweaty pullover and call Paul.

His jeep rumbles into the garage as I pull two beers from the fridge, popping their tops and bringing them to the coffee table, flipping the deadbolt switch open on my way. He bounds up the steps, flings the door open and crosses our living room in four easy steps, pulling me into his arms and taking my mouth.

His mouth is desperate on mine, like he has been away a month instead of a day. He spins me around and sets me down, his eyes lingering on me before he wheels around and shuts the door.

We eat on the couch, sharing the sandwich, juice running down my wrist as I try to bite into the overfull sandwich. I get up twice for napkins and more beer, our conversation dancing over, but not touching, my activities last night. Paul prefers to not discuss the existence of Stewart. While Stewart approaches their shared split of my time as he would a business merger—coolly and unemotion-ally—it is much harder for Paul. I have all of Paul's heart, surfing and his career taking a backseat to me, to my happiness. I'm sure he struggles with that—having half of me while giving me all of him.

But I was with Stewart first, gave him that half of my heart before Paul ever came into the picture. Initially, Paul was just sex to me, a warm body to fuck and occupy my days while Stewart worked. But... somewhere, over a year ago, Paul took the other half of my heart, and I fell for him as well. I know it bothers Paul. I know he is competitive and possessive and wants me to be only his. But he won't give me up over that desire, so he doesn't fight it. He goes with the flow and only asks for my happiness.

We eat, we watch tv, and then fuck—starting in the cramped shower and taking the activity to our bed. Then we spoon and the sound of waves lulls us to sleep.

24

DANA

A secret. Something not meant to be known by others.

What do you do when you discover a secret? Do you have a responsibility to share it? Or is the responsibility in the keeping of the secret?

I think it all depends on the outcome of sharing the secret. Some cause harm, some good. I need to find out more about this secret. To know what outcome it harbors. So, I will watch and try to find out as much as I can about this woman. Try to find out why she has latched onto these men, who hold my heart as much as she holds theirs.

I don't know if she loves them or is toying with them. The chances of both of us loving them are too slim, too incredible to be a coincidence. What I don't understand is why. Why these two men?

With the millions of men in Los Angeles, why date brothers?

25

HOLLYWOOD, CA

MADISON

I watch Stewart sleep, following the strong rise and fall of his chest. He is so rarely still. Intensity is his standard, so I enjoy seeing his rare moments of peace. At a time like this, when his eyes are closed and his breathing is soft, I feel protective of him. As if I have some responsibility for his world, for his happiness, for his life.

I love him, there's not been a question of that for some time. I fell quickly for this brilliant man—a man who has no time for anything more than quick minutes of affection. He will never bounce our child on his knee or take me to the doctor when I am sick. Those are his limitations, and he realizes that—is regretful for that short-coming but unwilling to change. He has chosen his lifestyle, and accepts the restrictions that come with it. Maybe one day he will change. Maybe one day his brow will relax, and he will smile easily, laugh more often, and lose the suit and tie. Maybe he will be able to do more than fuck me senseless and kiss me before leaving me alone. Maybe he will have a life outside of work, and maybe I will still be around when that time comes.

Life is too unpredictable to plan for that. What I do know, as I watch this beautiful man sleep, his face relaxed and body still, is that I love him. Just as much as I love Paul.

And one day, that will be a problem.

26

10 YEARS EARLIER

A wave of heat pushed Jennifer Brand back from the fire pit, her feet sinking in the thick sand. She tripped, stumbling backward, and was caught by strong arms, her gaze looking up and catching on gorgeous green eyes and a cocky smile.

"Gotcha."

She blushed, gripping his forearms and pulled herself to solid sand, brushing off her legs. "Thanks."

"It's Jen, right?"

"Jennifer." She hated Jen, hated the childish lilt of the name.

"Cool. Having fun?"

She nodded enthusiastically, her eyes drawn to his body, to the ripped six-pack he proudly displayed.

"We were actually about to head over to a house party over in Summerset. You seem pretty cool ... you wanna come?" He flashed a smile that any warm-blooded teen would be crazy to resist, one that displayed his dimples to perfection.

Yes, I would love to come. I would love to do anything you ask. She hesitated. "I've got to ask my brother, I came here with him."

He stiffened slightly. "Really? Who?"

"Paul Brand."

He stepped back a pace, surprise on his face. "Really? You're Paul's little sister?"

Nodding, she blushed at the impressed look he shot her. "Yeah. It's my birthday ... so he brought me along."

His look turned wary. "Eighteenth birthday?"

"Yeah," she lied. "The big one."

He nodded with a smile. "I knew your sister, Dana. You look a little like her. Prettier." He flashed another smile, this one a little awkward, as if he regretted the comment. There was a shout, and he turned, waving absently at a group that passed. "Well ... ask your brother. Summerset party. We can drop you wherever when it's done. And tell him I'm a fan. He's lethal on that board."

Stuffing her hands in the front pockets of her jean skirt, she nodded, watching his profile as he turned and jogged through the sand, effortlessly catching a beer that was tossed his way. Then she glanced around, looking for Paul.

He was by the dunes, his body wrapped around a girl she couldn't really see. She hung back, unsure about interrupting, glancing back at the fire before hesitantly calling his name.

There was a groan from the two bodies, and a muffled whisper. Paul climbed to his feet, his back to her, his hands adjusting the front of his swimsuit before he turned, his face an irritated expression. "What's up, Jennifer?"

"I'm ready to leave." The words spilled out without premeditation, but she saw the brilliance in them as soon as they came out, Paul's expression fighting hard to disguise his frustration.

"Now? We haven't even been here an hour."

"I know. There is a big group headed to Summerset to hang out. I could go with them—you could just pick me up there when you're ready to leave here." She said it casually, as if she didn't care either way. As if her entire love life wasn't resting on his answer.

His eyes lit up. "Really. Summerset? Who all's going?"

"Just some girls I've been talking to. It's a big group. I'll be safe."

The girl in the sand called out his name, and he glanced back for a moment, indecision in his eyes. "You got a cell on you?"

She rolled her eyes. "Yes. I have my cell, and I'll be with a group. It's just like any other night I go out. Mom and Dad would be fine with it. Just call me when you leave here. You can pick me up then."

He looked back once more, then studied her face. "All right. Just be safe. I love you."

She grinned. "I love you, too. Thanks."

He stepped back, watching her closely. "Cell phone. Don't lose it and make sure the ringer's on. I'll call you in about an hour."

She waved, turning and jogging up the beach toward the fire.

"Happy Birthday!" he called out after her.

She waved again, without looking back, her eyes skimming the fire-lit bodies, looking for the athletic build of her dreams.

He had a football in hand, and was heaving it into the darkness, a dim figure in red jumping up to catch it. She jogged up, tugged gently on his shirt, and waited for him to turn. He did, throwing an arm around her shoulders and pulling her to his chest. "You coming?"

"Yeah. If that's still okay." She beamed up at him.

He squeezed her shoulder gently. "More than okay. Come on, you can ride with me."

He whistled to a group, the guys turning, ditching red cups into the nearby dunes, insults and laughs tossed out as they dispersed.

Five minutes later, she was lifted into the backseat, his strong hands lingering on her waist, then sliding the seatbelt across her lap, teasing her bare thighs as it moved. He clinched the buckle, his face close to hers, and leaned forward, pressing his lips against hers.

He leaned back, breaking their connection. "At the party, stick close to me. I'm gonna need more of that."

His words made her smile, her cheeks warm, her lips still tingling from his kiss. "Okay."

He tapped the roof. "Let's go!" he yelled.

She glanced at the boy next to her, extending a shy smile. "Hi."

The guy smiled, all ruddy cheeks and thick black hair. "Heard you're Brand's sister."

She nodded.

"He's sick on a gun. Everyone knows who he is."

"He taught me how to surf," she offered.

"Hey!" The loud voice from the front seat broke their conversation. "You hitting on my girl, Brian?"

"Just making conversation, Jason," the boy muttered, grinning at her.

My girl. She bit her lip to contain a smile, grabbing the armrest as the truck was slammed into drive, throwing her slightly forward.

27

10 YEARS EARLIER

DANA

LOS ANGELES GAZETTE

PRESS RELEASE: LOS ANGELES COUNTY

A late night of partying and drinking has taken the lives of three Los Angeles residents, one of them a seventeen-year-old girl. The driver, Jason Tate, is in critical condition at Long Beach Memorial Hospital and had a recorded BAC of 1.23.

Tate's vehicle, a 1992 Land Rover Defender, lost control on Pacific Coast Hwy at approx. 11:14pm on Friday evening. The vehicle crashed through a guardrail before rolling down a steep embank. Jason Tate, a 21-year old UCLA student, was thrown from the vehicle and suffered severe head trauma. The bodies of Brian Jesup and Jennifer Brand were found in the burnt-out vehicle, restrained by seat belts. It is unknown if they were conscious when the vehicle caught fire, the blaze a result of the impact, which cracked the fuselage and tank.

The third fatality, Robert McCormick, was found a short distance from the vehicle, and died of head injuries.

A joint memorial service will be held on Saturday at 2pm. In lieu of flowers, please make donations to M.A.D.D. of Los Angeles.

That night ripped apart our lives. I came home, leaving Berkeley mid-semester, and found Mom on her bedroom floor, sobbing, her arms wrapped around a framed photo of our family. It was one taken before Dad's heart attack, back when we were a family of six. He'd passed and we became five. Lost Jenn and became four. Within a few more years, we were only three. Three separate souls, unconnected except for the blood in our veins and love locked away in the stubborn places of our hearts.

"She was seventeen!" Stewart yelled, pushing Paul against the wall, frames rattling from the impact. He dug his hands into Paul's shoulders, their faces only inches apart. "Seventeen!"

"She wanted to go. I didn't know. I thought it was just a party." Paul's words stumbled out of his mouth, a sob thick in the back of his throat, his body slumping down the wall as Stewart released him.

"Did you put her in the truck?" Stewart asked, every word a bite of venom. "Did you look into the eyes of the boy who killed her? Or were you too busy fucking around to worry about something as simple as our little sister's life?"

Paul was silent, his head in his hands, shoulders racking as he tried to contain silent sobs.

"You fucking disgust me," Stewart said, breathing hard, his face tight with barely restrained rage. I left my post by the wall, stepping forward, my eyes meeting Stewart's for a fraction of a second before I wrapped my arms around his chest. He gripped me tightly, so tightly it hurt, his need so great, his heart openly breaking between my arms. "She's gone," he whispered, his voice gravelly. "She's fucking gone." His voice broke, and I felt the shake of him, his strong frame crumbling in my arms, his breath gasping as he buried his face in my hair. "What the fuck are we going to do?"

I held him, my own tears flowing, my eyes blocked from Paul by the wide expanse of Stewart's chest. I wanted to go to him, to hug my little brother, but could feel the anger radiating from Stewart, mixing with his pain, the combination crippling him. I pulled back, looking up into his eyes. "Mom's asking for you."

He nodded, squeezing me one final time before stepping away, his eyes never going to Paul, his profile furious.

I waited until he left the room, slamming the door shut with a finality that hurt, then hurried to Paul and crouched next to him. I wrapped my arms around his shoulders, squeezing tightly as I felt him shake. When he sat up against the wall, his wet eyes staring straight ahead, I curved into him. "He hates me," he whispered.

"He's just in pain," I said softly. "He'll change, Paul. He knows you tried to do the right thing."

"I didn't. I was being fucking selfish," he choked out. "I should have been with her. It was her birthday. It's my fucking fault." He gripped my forearm and rested his head on mine, letting out a shuddering breath. "It's my fucking fault, and he knows it. He *should* hate me."

"He doesn't hate you. He loves you." I hoped desperately it was the truth. But what if Stewart loved Jennifer more? And when one love kills another, can you still love the one who's left?

Stewart left immediately after the funeral. He and Paul didn't see each other for three years—until Mom's funeral. They framed her casket, two handsome profiles in black suits with somber faces. Then, the separation continued. It has been seven years and three months since her death. Seven years of silence.

The first few years, I ran ragged between the two of them, attempting reconciliations. I sweated over holidays, birthdays, lunches. But they never yielded and time only increased the distance. After years of trying to maintain my relationship with both of them, Paul asked me to stay away. He said it was too painful to see my face, that I reminded him too much of her. I fought it, continued to try. But then he changed his number and moved. The disconnected phone and empty apartment made his feelings crystal clear.

Now, Paul has to understand that we can't control everything, that sometimes terrible things just happen. Stewart had been cruel, burying him so deep in guilt that it took years for Paul just to smile again, to realize he is a good person who made a simple mistake. I think he now begrudges Stewart for those years of pain, when he was close to suicide over the loss of his sister and the guilt he felt.

The last time I spoke to Stewart, he was still bitter at Paul for Jennifer's death, and too proud to admit anything to the contrary.

They both loved their little sister so much. That love made her death impossible to recover from, at least where their relationship was concerned.

Which is why the present situation is so precarious. Another woman holds both of their hearts in her hands. Their relationship didn't survive Jennifer, I'm worried their hearts won't survive this woman.

I *have* to protect them. I'm their sister, it is my duty.

28

VENICE BEACH, CA

MADISON

The alarm chirps in our silent bedroom, soft yet insistent, my hazy mind deciphering sleep from reality. Paul groans, and the bed shifts as he rolls over and fumbles for the clock, knocking something off the beside dresser. Silence. I lie still and try to figure out what, where, and why the alarm would be going off.

Ugh. It comes to me. Mother. I sit up, my head aching, a painful reminder of what late night poker, cigar smoke, and too much Miller Lite can do. Paul reaches for me, and I lean down, ignoring the scream of pain in my head, and kiss his forehead. "Go back to sleep. I've got brunch with Mom."

"Have fun."

I playfully bite his earlobe, harder than necessary, and he grunts in response, pulling the covers over his head. I head to the kitchen first, desperate for aspirin.

I dress for my Mother—a long sweater over a shirtdress. Boots. My hair twisted into a chignon. As I drive, I prepare myself for the inquisition that awaits me. Even though she has destroyed her own life, she still considers herself the foremost authority on my future, and will spend every moment of the upcoming event to make sure my life is on the proper track. Parental guidance marinated in bourbon.

I approach the manicured lawns of Beverly Park a half-hour ahead of schedule, my convertible slowly winding through the familiar roads of my childhood. I have a brief moment of nostalgia for my diamond-encrusted upbringing, familiar homes and restaurants reminding me of shopping, teenage groping over the gearshifts of Ferraris, and spring break trips to Europe. I turn into the large gates of Maurice's neighborhood and roll down my window.

"May I help you?" This neighborhood doesn't believe in rent-a-cops. They employ off-duty police officers, give them crash courses in overkill, and then post them, like sentries, outside of million-dollar gates.

"I'm here to visit Evelyn Fulton. My name is Madison Decater." I pass him my identification and ignore the death stare he sends my way. He checks my trunk, a minuscule space barely big enough to hold a case of beer. We go through a song and dance where he quizzes me on my mother's address, verifies I'm not staying for longer than four hours and confirms that Maurice and Mother are expecting my arrival. It's a good thing I'm ahead of schedule. Heaven forbid I miss a moment of brunch.

The gates finally open, the guard fixing me with a glare of the Brock Lesnar variety. I give him a cheerful wave and crank up the radio, pulling forward with a gentle squeal of tires. Five minutes later, I'm lost.

Fuck. I stare at the giant Mediterranean villa before me. All of these homes look alike. Huge. Tile roofs. Palm trees. Dollar signs. When one home got a private gated entrance, they all did, the constant need to one-up each other steamrolling into a giant ball of *allourhouseslookthesame*. I've only been here a handful of times, my avoidance of Mother's new life a dedicated one. It's been six months since my last visit, long enough to erase my compass.

I repeat the address in my head, reversing the car and looking for a street sign. There's nothing. This ridiculous neighborhood doesn't believe in street signs or house numbers, something so ghastly as numerical digits having no place in their architectural façade. I fumble with the GPS and glance in my rear view mirror, terrified that flashing lights and an overzealous security guard will appear and start another round of questioning. I zoom in on the map and see my car in the middle of nothing, a blue dot in the midst of brown dirt. I grit my teeth and call Mother's cell.

"You're late."

"I'm lost. Your neighborhood refuses to make any helpful overtures when it comes to directing strangers."

She sighed. "Where are you?"

I look at the house before me, barely visible behind the large gate and landscaped foliage. Then pull slightly forward, to a slightly different gate, with another well-hidden home. "I see gates. Big ass gates and little bits of home."

"Watch your language, Madison. I did raise you to be a lady."

I avoid that conversational landmine, driving farther, until I see a house that is actually visible, behind yet another imposing iron gate. "I'm in front of a white house. Spanish style, with an orange tile roof."

She huffs impatiently into the phone. "You know, the food is getting cold. And I don't have every home in this neighborhood memorized. Our house faces west, and we are in the back of the neighborhood. I'll send one of the help down to stand by the gate."

The help. I bite back a response. "Thanks, Mom. I'll be there soon." Movement catches my eye as I end the call as a white SUV pulls up behind me, its roof flashing red and white. I let out a groan, watching the door open and a uniform emerge.

29

BEVERLY PARK, CA

I watch my mother carefully and notice the slight tremor in her hand as she reaches for her drink. She smiles politely at her husband, and it's the sort of smile you give an acquaintance, not a loved one.

I don't mind Maurice. In terms of a husband, she could have done worse. He's polite, respectful, and puts her on a pedestal her beauty dictates but her behavior doesn't deserve. Maurice belongs to the proper clubs, has the acceptable balance sheet and gives her complete freedom, not that she uses it for anything other than drinking.

But he's ancient. Oxygen-mask, Depends stuffed in his nurse's apron, might-not-make-it-to-Christmas, ancient. And Mother, despite the tremor in her voice and her inability to do anything other than mourn her past life, is beautiful. Half natural-beauty, half enhanced by the team of world-class plastic surgeons she has employed her entire life. She looks thirty-five, with smooth skin, cosmetically perfect bone structure, and a body that most twenty-year-olds would kill to have, myself included. I don't know why she fights so hard to keep up her appearance, since she never leaves this house or visits the country clubs or the restaurants they could buy ten times over.

All of her friends abandoned her when our money ran out. I think she expected them to come back when she married Maurice, welcoming her back into their perfect little fold. But Mom was tainted, and when she fell from grace, it was a drunk belly flop in the middle of a sewage pond.

1. A drunken wander through the Spring Charity Gala, eating off of strangers' plates.
2. The eviction notice on the front door of our home, the grass overgrown, our car repossessed.
3. My exclusion from the debutante ball.

They'd seen her at her weakest and wanted no part of her return, despite the new wardrobe and prestigious address that accompanied it.

"Have you given any thought to returning to school?" Mother's voice interrupts my depressing walk down memory lane, her critical gaze cutting me from across fourteen feet of fine dining.

"No." Short and sweet is the best approach with her. It is likely she won't remember this meal tomorrow.

"And why not?"

"I have a job, Mother. I am doing just fine."

"Still single?" she asks, her perfectly waxed eyebrow raised.

My relationship status is her gauge of my personal success. If I had a wealthy boyfriend with husband potential, she'd cross me off her 'things to worry about' list, however short it may be. In her mind, a man who will take care of me is all I need. Whether or not love is involved is a moot point.

"Yes, Mom. Still single."

I'm not going to go into my dual relationship status with her. Not in front of Maurice, and not when our mother-daughter chats are spread six months apart. It's easier to listen to her lecture me about my singleness than hear her reaction to the truth. And if I only told her about one, then she'd want to meet him. I can barely handle brunch, much less a Chanel-clad zombie, playing the role of Dutiful Mother for an afternoon before being driven back to her alcohol-infused life. I love my men too much to make them go through that.

"Do you need money?"

She's noticed my car. The clean lines of my clothing, the Chanel J12 watch that decorates my wrist. She knows I don't need money, but I think the offer makes her feel superior. It's proof she has succeeded, pulled her life together and risen from the ashes of my father's crash.

"I don't need money, Mom. I'm good."

Maurice interrupts our awkward exchange, asking about books, and our brunch takes a pleasant turn as we discuss the latest bestsellers and our thoughts on them. Maurice is a reader, his library one that I drool over. I'm talking fourteen-foot ceilings, worn paperbacks and hardbacks filling deep bookshelves that take up three walls and reach to the ceiling. I've spent hours curled into the deep leather chairs in front of the fireplace, a stack of books before me. It is where I escape during holidays, parties, and any other occasion that dictates my presence in this household.

After the table is cleared and Mother switches from mimosas to Arnold Palmers, I help Maurice to his feet, and we make the long and slow journey to the library. I've brought a stack of new hard-covers that fit his taste in reading. We sit down by the fireplace, and I walk him through the selection, stacking them in the order that I think he'll prefer.

Then we read in companionable silence for two hours, until I notice the time and stand to leave. I walk over to Maurice, who has fallen asleep, his head tilted back at an awkward angle. Tiptoeing around him, I gently place a small pillow under his head and lightly kiss his cheek. I may not love the old man, but I do appreciate him, and am grateful that my mother has someone to take care of her, even if I don't understand the dynamics of their relationship. At a certain age, I think loneliness is the biggest battle to fight, and I hope my inebriated mother at least provides companionship for him.

I find my mom in the front parlor, sitting back in a chair, also asleep. I set a book next to her, the last one in my bag, a romance I know she'll enjoy. I head for the front door and smile at the uniformed maid who holds out my jacket. "Thank you. Please thank them for the brunch."

She nods politely and opens the door for me. I take one last glance at my mother and then step out, the cool spring air reminding me of the jacket in my arms. I shrug into it and jog down the steps to my car, ready to get back home.

Life in luxury can be stifling.

30

VENICE BEACH, CA

I walk into our home and am greeted by the delicious view of Paul's backside, a wet suit unzipped and hanging from his hips, baring his upper body and hiding his bottom half in skintight vinyl. He turns, a bowl of Kraft Mac & Cheese in hand, a spoon halfway to his mouth.

"Back so soon?" he asks through a mouthful of food, setting the bowl on the counter and pulling me into his chest.

I resist the urge to push him off, the damp feel of him sinking through my clothes, the scent of salt water hitting my nose. "It was a quick visit—one to appease my mom before their trip to Italy." I smile up at him, and let out a laugh when I notice the insistent bulge in his wetsuit, poking against me. I drop my bag on the floor and wrap my arms around his neck. "God, you are impossible."

"What can I say? I'm addicted." His words are so sweet and sincere that they tug my heart. I tug on the zipper of his suit and drag it down. He pulls my mouth to his and walks me backward until I hit the counter.

I pull him out, the weight and rigidity of him beautiful, causing a weight in my pussy, a need in my core. His kiss softens, dipping slowly into my mouth as he thrusts forward with his hips, his cock sliding in and out of my hand, the wetsuit's slick vinyl cool and itchy against my thighs.

"You're wet," I whisper, coming off his mouth.

"So are you," he replies, pressing forward and pinning me against the wall as he takes another taste of my mouth.

It's a fact I can't deny, my panties sticking to me as he pulls up my dress, the thin material contrasting with the cashmere sweater that I wear over it. I move his cock, placing it between my legs, my boots putting me at a height that makes us fit perfectly together, the slow in and out of his bare thrusts creating a delicious friction between my legs.

"I love you." He pulls at the pins in my hair, loosening the updo and stares into my face as the slide of his cock draws a long pull of pleasure against my clit. "I need you."

"I need you, too. Right now." I'm getting the full brute of his ocean-blue eyes, flecks of gold in his hair, bleach blond brows furrowing as he squeezes my cheeks, pulling my pelvis tight to him, the fit of us causing his breath to hiss.

"As you wish," he growls, lifting up with his hands. My legs leave the floor and I shriek with surprise. With me in his arms, he kneels and lowers me to the kitchen floor. Setting me gently on my back, the hard floor cushioned by my sweater, his hands pull my dress up and slide my panties to the side, a finger slipping into me, his eyes lighting up at the touch.

Then he is back inside me, fucking me on the floor, our legs a mess of boots and bare feet, his wetsuit rubbing roughly against my legs, but I don't care. I don't care about anything other than the perfect, slick pattern he is thrusting into me. He stares down at me, his face framed by the flex and pull of his shoulder and chest muscles as he dominates me.

It's fast, it's messy, our bodies bouncing in unrestrained passion, his breath hard on my skin. He rolls, keeping me inside of him, and I'm now hot. I yank at my sweater, getting tangled in it, and he helps me battle with it, pulling my arms free. I grin, his playful smile matching my own, and his length twitches inside of me, a subtle hint for me to move. I lean forward, resting my hands on his chest and ride him.

It's work, my thighs burning, my hands digging into his shoulders, my breath coming hard as I slide up and down on him. His hands run lightly over my breasts, a tickle of pleasure, and I stare down at him, memorizing the intense burn of his gaze, the half open gape of his mouth, the strong frame of his body. I come close, then lose it, my thighs tiring and he takes over, holding me in place and pumping his hips up into me. It comes, hard and fast, my body tensing as I babble out a stream of nonsense, one that begs him not to stop, then break into a silent shudder.

He comes. *I love to hear him come.* He's vocal, moaning my name as he thrusts hard and deep, his arms tight around my body, his actions almost frantic in their movements. He needs me. He loves me.

He stills his hips, reaching up and pulling my hair to one side, his mouth soft against my skin as he kisses my collarbone. I close my eyes, enjoying the trail of his fingers against my skin, his cock getting soft inside me, the cool air from the open window floating over my bare ass.

I love him, and I need him too.

31

HOLLYWOOD, CA

My relationship with Stewart is a catch 22. If he didn't work, or didn't have a slave's addiction to the work, our relationship would be a success. We would have a fabulous sex life and the relationship to accompany it. We would drink champagne in bed and stay up late discussing our futures and pasts. We would spend weekends in bed and vacation on islands. We would have children and argue over bedtimes and house rules.

But all that isn't possible because of his full-time mistress: work. And if he weren't married to his work, if he was a normal man with free time and a clear mind, then he wouldn't be my Stewart. He wouldn't have the same intensity, the confidence, and satisfaction that he gets from his job. He *is* the job. His entire being, the traits that I love, are all cultivated and created on that phone through deals and negotiations. Stewart without his single-minded devotion to deals ... I wouldn't even know that man. He would be a stranger to me. And if I had a full-time Stewart, then I wouldn't have Paul. A full-time Stewart wouldn't require Paul. A full-time Stewart would want me all for his own.

He wakes me with his mouth and interrupts a dream that I gladly surrender. His mouth awakens my passions as well as my body, and he claims me, sliding his warm body atop mine, nudging my knees apart and grinding his body against me, the smooth slide of naked skin causing me to shiver beneath him. His cock grows hard between our bodies, and we are both ready when it bumps lower, thrusting inside of me.

It is the perfect way to wake up, the perfect way to start my day. Stewart knows what I need, knows the insatiable pull within me. And, wrapping my arms around his neck, I let him fulfill me.

~

Fourteen hours later, he drives, his hand loose on the gearshift, the car taking the tight curves of the road with ease. He drives like he does everything else: intently, with an edge of recklessness barely restrained by tight control.

I lean back, letting my head drop against the headrest and run my fingers gently over his forearm. His mouth turns up at the edges, a secret grin playing over his features. His hand releases the shifter and he turns up his palm, mine sliding into his, our fingers inter-locking.

He won't tell me where we're going. He just waltzed in the condo, catching me mid-bite on the white leather couch in the foyer, the couch I'm not supposed to eat near, a Dorito filling up my mouth, Coke balanced precariously on the sofa's arm. He shot the soda a bemused glance and grabbed my hand, pulling me to my feet, the bag of Doritos dropping to the floor. "I want to show you something."

And now we are driving through the dark. Leaving downtown and taking the freeway east, toward the ocean. I crack the window slightly and let a burst of fresh air inside, Stewart promptly rolling the window back up. I sigh, watching as the exterior slows and the car turns into a residential area.

"Are we visiting someone?" Stewart and I don't socialize outside of business functions. Unlike Paul and I, we don't have friends or acquaintances. We exist in our own bubble of two, our time together too short to share.

"Just be patient." He pulls out his phone, checks an email, then looks up. "Look for Palm Drive." The car slows, and he rolls the windows down, squinting down dimly lit streets.

"Right there." I point ahead. "To the left."

We turn, he looks at his phone again, and then we make the final, undercarriage-scraping turn into the empty driveway of a one-story bungalow, Spanish-style white, blue shutters framing its front windows. He puts the car in park, and I wait, confused, glancing out at the dark house, no lights on inside.

"Let's go in." He unbuckles his seat belt and opens the door.

The front door opens with a key Stewart produces from his pocket. He leaves me in the foyer and walks through, flipping on lights as he moves, illuminating marble floors, a chef's kitchen, a fireplace built into the far wall. My sense of unease grows until he finally reappears, standing before me and spreading his arms proudly. "So? What do you think?"

I step toward him, glancing around. "I'm a little confused. Are you moving?" I know he's not. He can't. The ten-minute commute would drive him crazy—thousands wasted in those precious minutes spent on something as trivial as transportation.

"It's for you." His smile falters slightly at my expression. "Don't you like it?"

"But I already have a house." *With Paul.* The words that don't need to be said.

"You *rent* a house. In a section of town that has the crime rate of Compton." His tone irritates me.

"I *like* where I live." *And whom I live with.* Paul would move, but only to make me happy. He wouldn't want to live in this manicured neighborhood of picket fences and paved drives. We've got to be thirty minutes from Venice. "I'm right by my work."

"Here, you'd be closer to me. And this is ten times nicer than where you live." He's right, though he's never been to our place. For all he knows, it has twelve-foot ceilings and five bathrooms.

I try to stay calm. "Have you closed on this?"

"No. It's closing in ten days. Sooner if you'd like."

No. I would not like. "Stewart, this is a very kind gesture, and I really appreciate the thought..."

"But you don't want to move." His face is unreadable, and I move to him and wrap my hands around his neck.

"No. I don't want to move. Can you pull out of the sale?"

He sighs, his hands sliding around my waist and slipping under the top of my jeans. He squeezes the top curve of my ass. "It's gonna be hard." He pulls me forward, pressing the length of my body against him, and my breath catches as he lifts up with his hands, pulling me tight to his pelvis.

"How hard?" I breathe.

He smiles against my lips and takes a deep taste of my mouth before pulling off. "Why don't you get on your knees and find out?"

I think it hurt his feelings, my refusal of his gift. But it was too much. Not the gift of the house—I'm not too proud to accept a million-dollar piece of real estate. But it hadn't just been a house. It would have been a change of my life. I love my time with Stewart. But the everyday with Paul? Waking up next to him in the house that creaks under our feet and has hosted our sex on every available surface? I love that part of my life. And all of it would change if we were to move into a house of Stewart's. It would shift the entire dynamic of our relationship.

Sex soothes Stewart's hurt. It heals his ego, and he earns every ounce of it back. Making me scream his name, my body bent over, gripping the granite countertop, his hard cock claiming me from behind. On my back in the master, my legs spread before him, his hands lingering over my skin as he fucked me to a second, then—legs flipped over and my body on its side—third orgasm. We finished on the back deck, the night air cool on our hot skin, his breath labored as he kissed the length of my skin, his hands following his mouth, making a final exploration of my body, pushing me down to my knees.

We christen the hell outta the house, despite my lack of future inside it. Then we turn out the lights and Stewart locks the door with one last, regretful look inside. "You sure you don't want to sleep on it? Ashley will be so disappointed, she thought you'd love it."

"Then you can buy it for her," I tease. "But no. I'm sure."

He snags my arm and presses me against the door, taking one more possessive, full-body taste, his mouth aggressive as his hands take a long survey of my body. When he finally releases me, I stay against the door, looking up into his face, partially in shadow, his looks no less devastating in the dark.

"Thank you. For thinking of me."

"I love you. I want you to be taken care of."

I smile. "I am. I don't need a house for that." I stick out my tongue playfully, and the serious moment is broken. He tugs at my hand, and we return to his car, and then to his condo. Which we christen also—just for the hell of it.

A normal person would ask themselves who they prefer. If both
men were standing on a cliff, and I had to push one of them off,
who would it be?

But I'm not normal, and neither are they. Eventually, one of them
will tire of this relationship. One of them will want a full-time girlfriend or mother to his children. And then I will ask myself if that
is what I want. I'll ask myself if I can be happy with one man. If I
can be happy saying goodbye to the other man. And if those
answers are yes, then I'll go that path. It seems strange but, despite
their differences, there is a bit of each other in these men. And
even if I leave one, I will always have part of him in the other.

Paul knows that one day that question will come, and he avoids it.

Stewart doesn't have time to think about it.

32

VENICE BEACH, CA

DIDDY MOW: [NOUN]

**THE WORST KIND OF WIPEOUT. ONE THAT CAUSES
BROKEN BONES, MISSING TEETH OR LOSS OF LIFE**

The weather has turned and it's deceptive, the water sparkling, sun
bright. From the view, it looks like bathing suit weather, but the
draft feels like the open door to a fridge. I get out of bed shivering
and run through the house, working the rusty windows closed.
Diving back under the covers, I curl up tightly to Paul's warm body.
He mumbles something, his arms wrapping around me, and he pulls
me closer to his chest.

We wait until noon, when the sun has been out long enough to take
the chill off the day, and then head out, the initial shock of cold
water goose-bumping our exposed skin. After an hour, our muscles
are warm and we are contemplating the incoming waves.

I love the anonymity of being out here. The sand and water don't care if you are a spoiled rich kid or a foster child. The current doesn't yield to society's expectations or discriminate. And there is little you can buy that will improve your ride of a wave or lower your risk of death. In the water, we are all equal in the wave's eyes. All opponents that will either conquer the surf or succumb to it.

I rode a surfboard before I ever did a bike. The waxed feel of epoxy underneath my soles is as familiar as sand. I'm not Paul. I don't ride on the edge of death, don't tackle the monsters that rise to the height of a building and then crash down on innocent souls. I ride the waves I know I can handle and don't bite off more than I can easily chew. And this gradual curve that approaches, is a wave I can handle.

I watch it coming, feel the tug as it pulls from behind me, the subtle awakening of the surrounding water as we all prepare for its arrival. I glance around, Paul sitting up and gesturing for me to go, no other surfers around. A collision on a wave is dangerous, the hard impact of boards brutal at a time when the smallest mistake can mean danger.

I count the seconds, watching the curve of water, feeling the pull of current, and then lean forward, lying flat against the board, and paddle. Quick, strong strokes, the rush of excitement entering my muscles as I pick up speed.

It is coming.

I am ready.

33

PAUL

I love her. She knows it. I don't hide the fact. But I don't think she knows how *much* I love her. How my chest expands to a point of pain when she smiles. How I ache when I leave her, how my hands sometimes tremble when I finally get to touch her again. She is everything I don't deserve and everything I could ever hope to attain. I watch her, the glint of sun off her hair, her blue wet suit bending as she leans forward, her legs swinging onto the board, her movement as she paddles away from me.

Her hair is loose, long, wet, blonde tendrils, falling off her shoulders, her yellow board cutting through the water. The wave lifts me, coming in strong, my feet pushed and pulled as it moves by. I frown, not liking the kick of water that spins beneath my feet. It is stronger than it looked, deceptive in its strength. I narrow my eyes and watch her form, her graceful leap onto the board, her arms steadying out. My angel.

I see her form rise and fall, and then she is gone, hidden by the curve of the wave.

34

MADISON

The board vibrates under my feet as I move forward, getting my footing and balancing, my arms outstretched, legs bent. I hit my spot and feel the lift of the board. I lean a little right, the board responding, and we hit the swell and slide down, gliding along the surface, picking up speed, my hair whipping in front of my eyes, stinging my face. I bend deeper, resisting the urge to tuck my hair back, every movement on a board attached to consequences. Then the world tilts, this wave stronger and faster than I had expected. The board shoots from underneath my feet, and I am yanked by my ankle strap, my feet flying outward. Unforgiving water smacks against my back, a teeth-shattering impact, and I am yanked down, a stolen breath captured before I am engulfed by ice cold water.

White noise.

The current is strong, unexpectedly so, and I tumble, pulled underwater, my eyes blinking rapidly as I am tossed around—the rough push and pull of water disorienting me, my struggle against the current useless. My lungs are beginning to burn, panic setting in, and I'm being dragged by the tether attached to my ankle. I hope to God it's pulling me toward the surface. The board should float, that should be the direction up. But I'm caught in a rip current, and I should go limp, but black spots are appearing in my vision, my lungs stretching and bursting in my chest. I fight despite my training, and when my hand breaks into the air, and I kick hard, my foot unexpectedly free, and suddenly I have too much to process and not enough oxygen to react.

I realize it all a second too late. A second before my head breaks the surface, fins come slicing through the water, the yellow flash of my board, rubber-banding back, its recoil effect headed directly toward me.

Impact.

35

PAUL

I cannot see her. The wave came, she stood, she rode, and then she fell. We all fall. I fall into five-foot monsters, the kind that eat up and spit out surfers like gum. It is okay. She knows how to fall, knows what to do if the current pulls her under. Knows to go limp and let it spit her out. But this one had a strong kick. I felt its pull, worried over its strength. But still. She will find the surface. I'll see her bright yellow board, her mess of sunlit hair. I paddle forward, my gaze skimming over the surf, and another wave is coming, its back draw pulling me briefly away.

On the left, a flash of yellow. Her board, bobbing to the surface. I pause, searching carefully, then frantically, for a sign of her body.

Dark blue expanse, occasionally dotted by colorful bits of surfer. White foam, dark seaweed, her yellow board. Nothing else. Dark blue expanse.

Then I see her suit bob to the surface, facedown in the water, and my entire world ends.

I fly through the water, aided by the wave, and am at her side in seconds, flipping her over. Her body moves easily, without resistance. Without *life*. I pull her onto my board, and bend over her, undoing the velcro of her ankle leash, hesitating as I hold the cord. She will kill me if her board is lost. It's an extension of her, of her life on the water. We have fucked on these boards, kissed, dozed on them, and fought the demons in these waves. Then I push it aside and lean over her body. I pump at her chest, I breathe into her mouth, and I glance frantically to shore, struggling with the decision of whether or not to paddle her in.

It is a horrific decision to make. Continue working to save her life, or to take her somewhere where she might get more help. The shore holds paramedics, defibrillators, oxygen. Shore means at least two minutes of paddling. Maybe longer, my speed hampered by her additional weight on the board. I pray to a God I have ignored for too long and push air into her still mouth.

The first time I kissed her was on the roller coaster. Hard plastic underneath me, the scent of sunscreen coming off her skin, she had reached over and pulled me to her like it was nothing. Like it was natural that we would spend that moment, as strangers, exploring each other's mouths. She had been so gorgeous, so vibrant. It was like she had been so pumped full of life that it was spilling out, she overflowed with it. Just being with her—in line, on that ride, her hand in mine... it was intoxicating. That kiss was my first injection, and she became my addiction from that point forward. Addiction made me come back after she told me about the other man, broached the scenario where I would only own half of her heart. I mentally worked through it then, and I don't care now. I only need her in my life. The rest can be made to work.

It isn't working. I push harder on her chest, her wet suit slick beneath my palms, my movement awkward on the thin board, a large wave knocking me off balance when I lift from her chest. I look to shore and lay down, as gently as I can, atop her body, and paddle as fast as my arms will go.

I have paddled hundreds, if not thousands, of miles. Accelerated bursts of speed to catch up to a wave. Long sprints to race another surfer back to shore. But never has my stick moved this fast. I gasp for air, my heart squeezing in my chest as I move my arms, listening, straining my body for a hope of air, a movement in her limbs, a sigh. *Something.* I try to calculate time, to know how long it has been, but panic sets in, and I push those thoughts to the side. I notice the blood halfway to shore. Beads of liquid streaming down the board, coming from her head. *Do the dead bleed?* I scream, the shore approaching, and heads look up. Feet move along the sand toward us, and I clear the final distance until it's shallow enough to stand, and I sweep her cold body into my arms.

Her lips are blue. Her face is slack. I have failed her. I hold her tight to my chest and sprint out of the water.

36

HACK SHACK: (noun)

Hospital

PAUL

I have only ever loved four women in my life. The first two are dead. I've lost communication with my sister. I am praying fervently for Madd. The paramedics surround her, their red polos bent, voices crawling, and all I can see are her feet, sticking out, her toes pointing to the sky in an unnatural way. She curls into a ball when she sleeps, her feet tucked, her head often on my stomach or my arm, her mouth curved into a smile even when she is sound asleep.

I move closer and they push me aside, won't let me close enough to see, but I can hear their words. There is a siren in the distance, and all I can do is thank God that we are in Venice where there are medical staff present on the beach and ambulances just around the corner. Up in Lunada or out in Malibu it'd be me and a bunch of empty mansions, quietly watching her die.

There is a cough, and my heart leaps. More coughs. Hard, hacking sounds that she has never made. Her foot moves, and I pray it is her movement, and a medic didn't bump it. An engine rumbles, and I am pushed aside once again as an ambulance pulls onto the sand. The last thing I see is her limp feet as she is placed on a stretcher. They wouldn't load a dead person onto a stretcher, wouldn't send them in an ambulance.

Right?

I get the attention of an EMT, grabbing his arm when he shuts the ambulance doors. "I'm her boyfriend. Can I ride with you?"

The man turns, his thin face looking me briefly up and down. "They won't let you in the hospital without a shirt and shoes. We're taking her to Venice Regional. Why don't you grab some clothes for you and her? Just in case. Also, if she has any identification, numbers of friends and family... grab it and meet us there." He moves around me and opens the passenger door. I turn, slipping on the hot sand, and run past familiar faces, past a dread-headed stranger who is examining my board, jumping over a handrail and pounding down a path I've taken many times before. *With Madd and without her*. I round the alley corner and bump into a man's chest, stumbling past him, ignoring his curse.

Two blocks.

One block.

I'm taking the stairs, knocking over the ceramic frog that Madd brought back from Tijuana and grab the key and shove it in the lock.

Home. It will never be home without her. Even now, with her scent in the air, the sheets twisted from an early morning fuck, it feels wrong. I shut the door, not wanting to let out any of her air, and move to the counter, grabbing her keys, phone, and wallet. I am torn between wanting to examine every item, to grab her sweater and inhale her scent, and the urgency that pushes me forward.

She may be alive. She may die. I need to get to the hospital.

I grab a trash bag from underneath the sink and stuff the first two stacks of folded clothes from the top of the dryer into it. *Clothes folded by her, her hips swinging, horrible voice crooning out an eighties song as she quartered a shirt.* I shove my feet into flip-flops and run downstairs, pocketing the key and yanking the door shut behind me.

I break at least five laws to get to the hospital. I leave the truck under a red sign that flashes 'EMERGENCY ROOM' and grab her things, run into the lobby, and approach the desk.

She is alive.

It is the first thing I ask and is answered without hesitation, followed instantly by two words that make my heart drop and chest ache. "For now." I can't take this roller coaster.

The high and intense joy I hear at the announcement of her life.

Despair at the possibility that I might still lose her.

They won't let me back there. Not yet. Not until some future point that is not explained by the haggard receptionists. Then the door opens, and a woman in white steps out, her gaze finding me.

"Are you the boyfriend?"

"Yes."

She smiles and the motion doesn't reach her eyes. "She *is* breathing, but it's assisted. She's had pretty severe head trauma. That, combined with the six or seven minutes she was without air... we induced a coma until we can get her stabilized."

"Induced a coma? So, she can be brought out of it?"

She looks into my eyes. "*If* she still has brain function. She may be at a point where it's not feasible to pull her out of it. You should call her family, any close friends, and have them come here. She may not survive the night."

I ignore the sentence, even as it stands in the center of my mind and shouts, overpowering every thought process I struggle to have. "Can I see her?"

She glances at her watch. "They're working on her now. I'll have someone come out in about thirty minutes." She smiles grimly and turns, her coat flaring out, the white doors swinging shut behind her.

They're working on her now.

You should call any family or close friends.

I step forward until I am before a chair, and I turn, sinking into it, my hand loosening around her wallet and phone, the items sliding into my lap. *Call family or friends.*

Friends. Madd doesn't really have a lot of friends. We have a big group who we hang out with—several of the guys professionally surf, and all of the girls hang out together. But they're the type you call when you are five blocks away and have a flat tire, not when you're on life support and might not last the night. Madd and I could disappear from this stretch of beach, and it'd be weeks before anyone really noticed.

Family. Madd's entire family consists of one drunken individual. A mother who I vaguely remember being in Tuscany. Still, I could call her cell. I unlock her phone and scroll down the numbers, looking for 'M.' Just one contact line up from it, my breath stops.

LOVER.

Him. If I love half of her heart with my entire being, this man has a claim to the other half. The other half of the heart that is struggling to beat. I've seen his name displayed on her phone before, but never have I had the desire to call. I have no need to disrupt our life, no need to rock that boat. I know nothing about him. He may be married. Older. Younger. Black. White. He's wealthy, I know that. Her wrist and ears often glitter with presents, the new convertible in our garage is proof of that. I don't understand why any man would want his girlfriend to have another man in her life. It's either because he doesn't care about her—or because he loves her and knows she won't put up with being played with when he has time and otherwise ignored.

There is so much I don't know about this man, so much I never wanted to find out. Yet, here I am, staring at his name in her phone.

I'm torn. She's never wanted us to meet. She has this determined plan for our lives to play out separately, and it's worked for us so far. Now, I'm torn between respecting those wishes and knowing what I'd want, if I were him.

If I were him, I'd have to hold her warm hand in case it went cold forever. I'd have to hear her soft breath before it stopped.

If she wakes, she may hate me for it. But if she doesn't, I might not forgive myself for taking this moment from him.

37

PAUL

I press the CALL button and work through what to say, steeling myself for the unknown. I have no idea if he'll be friendly or a dick, and will be fucked if I have to leave a message. The female voice surprises me, chirping through the receiver with friendly efficiency. "Hey Madison."

I look at the phone, LOVER still clearly displayed on the front.

"Madison?" she repeats.

I clear my throat. "I was trying to reach..." I can't seem to formulate a single articulate sentence, and am stuttering over the fact that I don't know his name.

"Stewart? You were calling for Stewart?" the perky voice asks helpfully.

Stewart. That's his name. A name that inappropriately brings to mind visions of my brother's face. A brother I haven't thought of in some time. I swallow and return to the uncomfortable task at hand. "Yes. Is he available?"

"Mr. Brand is in a meeting right now. Does Madison need me to interrupt him?" Her tone is distractingly cheerful, so much that my brain takes a moment to catch up, to focus on the insanity that just left her lips.

"Mr. Brand?" My words come out unintentionally harsh. "Stewart *Brand?*"

"Yes. Is there a problem?"

My head comes up with a jerk. I hear her voice in my ear, the words fading into unintelligible forms. I drop the phone, spots appearing before my eyes, and I try to breathe, try to focus on what is before me and what is important. Madd. Lying a few walls away. *Dying.*

But my brain won't release itself, won't step away from the bomb that was just dropped in my lap. Stewart. My older brother. *Fucking* Madd. Touching her skin, holding her body, kissing her mouth. My brother. *He* is the one who has the other half of her heart. He is the one who I share her with. He is the one who dictated a second boyfriend. He is the one too busy to fully occupy her bed, her time.

Stewart.

My brother.

The one who beat up Noah Richardson when I was eleven because Noah wouldn't stop bullying me. The one who coached me through asking Nicki Farrahs out when I was too chicken. The one who explained sex and going down on a girl and who bought me my first box of condoms. The one who punched me in the face and blames me for causing our little sister's death. The one who told me never to step within a mile of him ever again. The one who wouldn't return my calls for five years, until I finally gave up and stepped away from the tattered remains of our family.

Stewart is *Him*. Stewart is LOVER.

The phone rings, and I glance down to his moniker displayed on the screen. Before I can second-guess the action, I scoop it up and hand it to the ER receptionist. "Please explain to them about Madison Decater," I request softly.

The woman shoots me a questioning look and then glances at the phone and flips it open. "Venice Regional ER," she says with efficiency into the phone.

I walk back to the chair and watch her face, watch her lips as they mouth words I can only guess. I wonder who is on the other end, if it is Stewart or the cheerful female. And I wonder what I will do when he walks through these doors.

Will she still be alive when he does?

38

STEWART

We are in the middle of a deposition, when Ashley steps in. I look up in warning, then see her face and hold up my hand, pausing the attorney mid-question. The transcriber looks up in surprise at the silence.

Ashley moves quickly to my side and leans forward, her lips close to my ear. "It's Madison. There's been an accident."

I close my eyes, unprepared for the words. *Not again.* Not after Jennifer. I stand and meet the attorney's gaze. "I have personal business to attend to. We'll need to reschedule."

"Personal business?" the bald man stammers. "Mr. Brand, it took a month to coordinate this."

I ignore him and follow Ashley out of the room, pulling the door to and turning to her. "Tell me."

My assistant, a cheerful sunflower with a spine of steel, is shaken. It is a look I have never seen on her, and the tremble in her voice terrifies me. "A man called from her phone. He wanted you, but hung up when I told him you were busy. It seemed odd, so I called back to get his name, a message, something. A woman answered, someone from the hospital. She said that Madison was in a surfing accident and is in a medically-induced coma. She said any close family and friends should come now." Tears well in her eyes, and she steps forward, touching my arm. "I'm so sorry, Stewart."

I brush off her contact. "Where's my phone?"

She passes it to me, and I try to sort through a logical thought process. "Get me a driver."

"Done. There's one in front. He has the hospital's address, and I've given the hospital your information."

I nod. "Also give them my American Express and have them charge me any medical expenses. I don't want any treatment or options unexplored due to cost. Make sure they understand that."

She nods, and a single tear drags down her cheek. She knows Madison well, has lunched with her countless times, chats with her in the reception area when my meetings run over. I manage an awkward hug and then head for the elevator.

We make the half-hour drive in fifteen minutes, my frustration at not having my car disappearing as soon as the driver makes the first hairpin turn at forty-five miles per hour. I cradle my head in my hands, visions of Madison assaulting me from all directions.

Her head on my pillow, a drugged smile on her lips when I kiss her goodbye in the morning.

The image of her in my t-shirt, cooking barefoot, nothing underneath but skin.

The small but firm push of her hands on my chest, her ability to weaken my resolve with one saucy smile.

I should have set aside my work, should have canceled meetings, planned vacations, made half the money and had twice the time with her. I should have taken her to dinner each night, been there for each birthday and holiday, met her mother, kissed her over breakfast, and told her how I felt. If she is gone, if I don't have a chance to say goodbye, she'll never know how I feel. How I cherish her.

I'm an idiot.

The car pulls up to the glass lobby, and I open the door, steeling myself.

She will be okay. She will live. I can make changes to our life. Marry her. Rebuild everything the way it should be, with her front and center.

I could fix this. I just needed another chance.

39

PAUL

Inhale.

Exhale.

Inhale.

Exhale.

I focus her breaths and examine the display beside her bed, the numbers foreign to me.

I run my fingers over the top of her hand—its cool surface scaring the hell out of me. I massage her fingers, the digits limp and unresponsive.

"There is brain activity."

I turn to see a young male nurse, outfitted in green scrubs.

He smiles. "Something came across the monitors a few minutes ago. It's a good sign."

"So, she'll be okay?"

His grin falters. "No. I didn't mean that. But with her condition… we didn't expect any brain activity. We're still a long way from stability."

I nod and turn back to her. Squeeze her hand again. No life. No response. I lean over and place a soft kiss on a bit of exposed skin on her cheek—tubes and masks preventing any real connection.

There's a commotion in the hall, and from the raised voices and the squeak of shoes on the floor, I know that Stewart is here. Without thinking, my hand tightens possessively on hers.

40

OVER THE FALLS: [phrase]

Getting pitched headfirst and slammed by the lip of a
crashing wave.

STEWART

The woman before me is infuriating. She blinks at me with steel-
gray eyes and purses her thin lips. "Only close friends and imme-
diate family may go in. She's in ICU and already has one visitor."

"I'm her boyfriend. Stewart Brand. My assistant should have called,
you spoke with her earlier."

"Her *boyfriend* is already in there. So, unless we have a love triangle
going on, I need to speak with him first. He's the one who brought
her in, and he's the one who has her identification."

I grind my teeth at the title, never regretting a single decision more
in my entire life than when I hear her reedy voice give ownership of

Madison to another man. "I don't need to explain the dichotomy of our relationship with you. Call Security if you wish, but I will be the one paying for her care and I—despite what you have been told —*am* her boyfriend. Her fiancé once she pulls through."

"*If* she pulls through." The woman's words are firm but gentle, the statement reminding me that Madison's health is more important than the cockfight I'm creating in my mind.

"I'll find her myself. Here's my card if you feel the need to get authorities involved." I flip a business card out between my fingers and set it on her desk. A nurse moves through the ICU doors and I push through the opening, and stride down the hall. I'm unsurprised when she follows, a clatter of shoes, sputtering as I glance in and out of rooms, ignoring the tug of her on my arm. I pass a room then stop, stepping back and glancing at the chart hanging on the door.

Madison Decater. Room F.

This is it.

I step inside and pull the door closed on the woman, the voices instantly muffled. There is a man beside her bed, his back to me. I ignore him, my attention focused on her, his figure muting in my peripheral vision, my horror growing as I see the frail figure who is my heart.

She lies in a hospital bed, her face covered with a breathing mask, tubes and cords running from portable stands to her body, face, and hands. The mechanical breathing of the machine is like a beast, wheezing out sounds that are nothing like her sweet sighs of sleep.

"My baby," I whisper. "Oh my God, my sweet, sweet girl." Tears spill. Tears I didn't even know my body could still create. I haven't cried since Jennifer, not even at Mother's funeral. But this, seeing her before me, struggling to breathe, artificially hanging onto life... it is as if I am seeing my life dissolve right before my eyes with no way of rescuing it. Her life, her fire... it's gone. It's gone, and I'm faced with the sudden reality that it may never come back. My mistakes will be etched in stone, unable to be wiped clean and rewritten. I sink to my knees beside her bed and pick up her hand, and it flops unnaturally. I pull it to my cheek, cradling the limp wrist, my breath gasping as I press soft kisses onto her palm.

I've known I love her. I've known that she is the light in my life and keeps my world from being too dark, too consumed with work. But I haven't known, haven't realized until now how my love for her works, how it is more than affection, how it is the only part of me that has life. She is the only feeling that exists in my body, the only feeling that isn't tied to greed or competition or ego. She is my light, and I haven't realized it until now, when it is so close to being extinguished.

I lay my head on her chest, and gently grip her to me. "I need you, baby. I love you so much."

There is a small cough, and I remember the other man in the room. The other man in her life. A man who, at this point in time, needs to take his leave, to step out of her life and allow me to take my rightful place. I gently release her and straighten, taking one long look at her before turning to face her other man.

⸻

Seeing Paul's face pulls the final nail from the coffin that is my sanity. He stands tall, taller than I remember, his chest strong, eyes fierce, blazing with the same passion I feel behind mine. I have seen his photo, Dana's letters occasionally containing a news article or magazine clipping. But a photo wasn't needed to know who he would grow into. I have memorized every line of his face since he was a child. Admired his athletic build, his skill in the water, his easy smile and infectious laugh. He was always our golden child, the one who talked his way out of trouble, rescued stray animals, and waltzed through life with an ease—just like Madison. The thought hits me hard, the similarities terrifying in their possibilities.

I freeze, examine the look in his eyes and try to piece the possibilities together, try to understand exactly what his presence means and pray to God it's not what it appears to be. "Why are you here?"

"The same reason you are." He nods toward the bed, toward the woman who I've spent the last two years thinking of as my own. I knew there was another man. Hell, I'm the reason she settled down with one. I didn't want her going home with strangers. I wanted to know she had a steady relationship, someone who'd watch out and care for her. I hadn't taken the time to consider that person having feelings for her, mentally claiming ownership of her. I've always pushed that reality to the side, work taking center stage, everything else flowing, the well-oiled machine silent enough to skip close examination. Realizing that *he* is her other man... Paul falls in love with baby kittens. I don't have to look in his eyes to know he's head over heels for her. Jesus Christ, I've fucked to the thought of her with him!

My legs lose all strength and my knees threaten to buckle. I stagger a few steps to the side and collapse into the closest chair, closing my eyes. There is a vibration in my pocket—my phone—and I reach in and hold the button on the side, depressing it until it vibrates and is off. "How long?" The words come out a whisper, and I clear my throat.

"The doctor should be back in about an hour with some results. We will know more then." I crack open my eyes to see him sit in a chair opposite me, leaning forward, his elbows on his knees, his eyes looking at her and then at me.

"No." My voice is stronger, though it still cracks as I speak. "*How long* have you been fucking her?" I open my eyes and look into his.

41

PAUL

My brother has changed so much. At twenty years old he was already serious, dedicated to school when I was partying, his brow furrowed over grades and projections, current events, and our family's finances. Worry, worry, worry at a point in his life when he should have been partying and fucking. Enjoying life. But he's even worse now. He's fully evolved into a rock hard frame of intensity. When he opens his eyes and stares at me, it is like being in the path of a train, frozen to the spot, unable to move even though the ground is trembling underfoot.

"A year and a half ... maybe two. We met in Santa Monica."

"So this... this is a coincidence?" Stewart's voice is hard and unbelieving, and it's through his petulant tone that I fully believe that this *is* solely happenstance.

I've worked through the scenario before he arrived, turning over the realization of his identity in my head and trying to figure out the pieces and what my part is in this twisted game.

I've decided there are three possibilities.

First. He sent Madd to me—some fucked up situation that reeked of anything but the levelheaded Stewart I once knew.

Second. Madd sought out two brothers, for reasons known only to her, a deceitful game that would only end in disaster. Also, completely opposite of the woman I love.

Third. It was all a coincidence. A fucked up, someone-upstairs-is-screwing-with-you, coincidence.

"It's either coincidence, or she somehow orchestrated this situation." I glance toward her bed. "And I don't think she would do that."

He drops his head back against the wall. "No. She wouldn't. Plus, I'm the one who pushed her to take a boyfriend."

"Why?" How could any man send Madison out into the world and not be concerned with the possibility of losing her? It's a question I've always contained, not wanting to rock the boat with Madd and a little scared at what the answer might be.

He sighs, keeping his gaze at the ceiling. "I assume you know how she is, with sex. From the beginning, I couldn't give her the time she needed. For sex or for a relationship. She deserved a full-time boyfriend and she knew it, refused to be exclusive with me. And…" He shrugged. "I couldn't stop thinking about her. I wanted her as a constant in my life, but I also wanted her to be safe, and happy, and loved. And… fuck. Satisfied. I didn't want her out fucking around. And I didn't want her out of my life." He pushes off the wall with his shoulder and sits up in the chair, meeting my gaze. "I thought if she had a man, someone to spend her days and nights with—someone who understood that I was there, that I had a place in her life—it would keep her happy and give me a spot in her life. Give our relationship some security."

I frown. "Without you… I could have had a normal relationship with her. *I could have made her happy.*" My voice strengthens, anger coursing through me. "I could have been everything she needed."

Stewart laughs, and the sound only pisses me off more. "You're a kid. You float through life in some imaginary world where you do what you love and are lucky enough to live off of it. But what are you going to do when you can't surf anymore? How are you going to provide for her? At some point you'll have to join the real world. And the real world *changes* people. The real world takes your cheery little smile and turns you in a dark cloud of reality. It drowns you in bills and expectations and adds pound after pound of reality on your shoulders until you're struggling under the weight of it all."

"So that gives you a permission slip to fuck with her life? Use her and then send her off when your cell phone rings?" I shake my head. "Fuck that. She's better than that. You were greedy and wanted to have her and work and I don't have to guess the order in which they stacked."

His features tighten, scowl deepening, and I want to punch him, like he did to me the night that Jennifer died. Ten years of resentment and anger boil, and my fists clench, my temper warring with my mind.

He snarls, uncoiling upright in the chair. "Paul, you're a *fuck* to her. Probably a good one. And you're fun. You've done a good job of keeping her company. But you can't be her everything. You're barely your own everything. And you'll fail her. Just like you failed Jennifer. Fuck—you were probably with her when this happened. Were you?"

He stands and moves close, his eyes dark, his jaw tight. "Were you *there* when she drowned? How many women who I love are you going to hurt with that casual attitude that lets everything important slip through the cracks?"

There's a level when your heart breaks past the point of repair, shattering into pieces that cannot be glued back together. His words are knives, the truth behind them lacing the blades with poison. At some point, I surge forward, my chest bumping his. But, halfway through his final words, when the truth and guilt burn into my soul, I weaken—and in the end, I drop to my knees, wincing when the final point hits its mark and bruises my soul.

I barely notice when he steps away and out of the door.

Inhale.

Exhale.

Inhale.

Exhale.

The mechanical breaths are the only sound in the room until I sob, crawling on my knees over to the bed and gripping the bars, heaving my weight up and leaning against her bed. "Please wake up," I plead. "Please, baby. *Please*. I love you and need you so much."

I need her fierce grip around me. Her playful gaze. The scrunch of her sunburnt nose. Her presence makes me feel invincible, as if all we have is golden time. No worries, no regrets. Two people running through life with our arms outstretched and the sun on our back. We don't need much. We have love. We will make everything else work. Fuck Stewart. Fuck him and his speech and his intensity.

How many women who I love are you going to hurt with that casual attitude that lets everything important slip through the cracks?

I love her.

I need her.

I need her.

I need her.

I sob and pray reverently—for forgiveness and for her.

Madison. My heart.

42

STEWART

I cannot go back in there. I cannot go back after the words I just said. I cannot face him after I saw the way his face crumbled. He's stood up to me so rarely in his life. And in there, in his anger and accusations, I saw the man he's become.

He was right. Without me and my selfish need to have her in my life, they could have had a normal relationship. Whether it had been him, or someone else, she would have found a normal life. Someone a hundred percent devoted to her rather than a job. Someone whose entire focus was making her happy, and who didn't divvy up her passion between two dicks. His words had hit home, and I'd pushed back with every pissed off bone in my body.

I can't go back in there. But she's in there, so I have to go back. I can't leave her alone, but I also can't face him again.

I am an asshole.

He is my brother.

She has my heart.

Fuck.

43

DANA

I am sipping artificially-sweetened strawberry lemonade and debating between a Caesar salad or tuna roll when my phone rings. I consider ignoring it. It's an unknown number, probably the office, and I don't feel like dealing with numbers and IRS regulations right now. I let it ring three times before my OCD gets the best of me, and I slide my finger across the screen. "Hello?"

"Dana. It's me." The catch in Stewart's voice has me instantly alert, and I push aside my excitement at hearing from him as panic grips my chest.

"What's wrong? Is it Paul?" I feel a tightness in my stomach I haven't felt in ten years, not since I was woken up by my mother and heard the news that broke apart our world.

"No. Yes." He inhales deeply, and I can suddenly see him, pinching the bridge of his nose as he struggles with whatever is about to come out of his mouth. "Paul is fine, but I need you. Can you come to Venice Regional?"

"The hospital?" I am on my feet and moving, my purse in my hand, abandoning my drink. I plow into the corner of a table and yelp at the stab of pain in my hip.

"Yes. How soon can you be here?"

Here. He's at the hospital. "*Is it Paul?*" I'd asked. No. Yes.

"Fifteen minutes. I'm in L.A. I moved back a year ago." I feel guilty saying the news, but it's not like he's answered any of my calls. It's hard to share information with a brick wall.

"I'll be in the ER lobby. Please hurry."

The phone goes dead in my hand, and I jog the remaining distance to my car, my heels clipping on the sidewalk as I stuff the phone into my purse. There is a moment of adolescent irritation that he didn't comment on my move, the slight replaced immediately by a sense of purpose. With his lack of availability, it didn't matter if I lived fifteen minutes or fifteen hours away. What *is* important is that he needs me, and that makes my heart beam. He needs some-one, and he called *me*. He said Paul is fine. Whatever is wrong, both of my boys are safe.

I get to my car and toss my purse into the passenger seat.

I see him as soon as I enter the lobby, his tall frame tense and hunched into a chair by the vending machine. He strides toward me and we collide, his arms encircling me, a tight kiss pressed to the top of my head.

"Let's step outside."

He speaks to the receptionist, who regards him with disdain, an odd reaction to Stewart's looks and traditional charm.

We step into the afternoon heat, and he stops by a bougainvillea and leans against a column of the overhang. "You got a light?"

"A cigarette?" I stare at him for a long moment before digging in my purse for a pack of Marlboros and a lighter. "What happened to your decade-long health kick?"

"It just ended." He taps one out and lights it, cupping his hand around the flame and inhaling deeply.

I take the pack from him and shake out another, stuffing the box back in my purse. "What's going on? As delighted as I am to hear from you, it's been three years."

He blows out a stream of smoke. "I know. You know what life's like. Time is gone before you even know it."

"Whatever." I snorted, lighting my own cigarette. "I don't think you have any idea what life's like. You know what work's like."

He's silent for a moment, staring out at the parking lot. Before us, a family of five barrel toward the door, faces grim, the youngest tripping over the curb beside us. I ignore the little girl, my attention taken by Stewart's turn toward me. He hasn't lost the intense gaze, that stare that cuts through any bullshit, managing to protect him while invading your soul.

"I need your help."

"Then talk to me."

He looks back out on the street, the whine of an ambulance coming closer. "It's about a girl."

Reality hits me like a fifty-pound wrecking ball, and I curse my own stupidity. *Duh.* I only know one fact about his current life. One blonde fact who prances between him and Paul. *Of course,* this is about her. How did it take me this long to see it? "*Is it Paul?*" No. Yes. I should have known the minute I got his call. "Go on."

"I'm in love." He brings the cigarette to his lips and sucked on the end, then flicked it to the ground. "She's amazing, D. She's amazing and beautiful, and I've screwed it all up."

I clamp my mouth shut, and hope that I look innocent.

"I was too busy. Working—you know my schedule. She wouldn't give me an exclusive relationship, not when I could only see her once a week or so."

I arch a brow and study his handsome profile, a sliver of respect reluctantly wedging its way into my hatred for the blonde. "Good. You don't have time for a house plant, much less a woman."

He stubs the toe of one glossy dress shoe on the cigarette. "I know. So, I told her to see someone else. I told her I'd share her. Told her to date him and me at the same time."

I almost blow my cover and say Paul's name. Almost. I swallow the words and aim for a casual tone. "*Share* her? With who?"

He shrugged. "I didn't know and didn't care. I just told her to find someone who made her happy. Someone who understood that I wasn't going anywhere."

"And you thought *that* would work out?" I stab the end of the cigarette onto the column and cross in front of Stewart, planting my feet and staring up into his face. "You thought what? She'd date both of you? Forever?"

He meets my stare solidly, and he's gotten some wrinkles around those eyes. They're faint but there, sandwiched in the lines of stress he always wears. "It was that or lose her. What was I supposed to do?"

I scoff. "Work a normal schedule. Cut back to sixty hours a week. Enjoy life. Have an actual relationship with someone, not timeshare her out!"

His face hardens, more lines forming. "I regret it now. I know I fucked up. But at the time—I didn't love her then. I had just met her. I didn't know where it would go."

I examine his face. "You *love* her." I test the words on my tongue, knowing, as my gaze moves over his features, that he means it. My big, strong, only-cares-about-work brother has fallen in love. The ambulance wail grows louder and I remember where we are standing. My blood chills. "Why are we here, Stewart? What happened?"

His face crumbles on the edges, a flash of weakness before he straightens, his defenses back. "There was an accident," he says. "A surfing accident. They don't think she's gonna make it."

A surfing accident. This situation suddenly has taken a nosedive into hell. I don't need to ask if Paul was there. I don't need to know the many parallels that must exist to tie this incident to the one ten years ago. I swallow hard, and my heart aches for my boys.

He wipes at his face, pressing his fingers against his eyes, and my desire to comfort him is overridden by my understanding that I should give him space. "Paul," he chokes out. "Paul was who she found. Talk about God fucking around in our lives. And when I found out... God, Dana. The things I said to him." He drops his hands and falls back against the column, staring out at the road, his eyes bloodshot, mouth grim. He suddenly looks old. Haggard. "How did this all happen?"

I wrap my arms around his waist and hug him tightly as I sift through everything he'd said. I'd had the entire situation wrong, had never dreamed that they were willingly sharing her.

I pull back and look up at Stewart. "Does he love her too?"

"He's Paul."

I understand instantly what he means. Paul loves freely and easily, accepting faults and unconditional in its strength. He wouldn't be with her if he didn't love her.

"Will you go talk to him?"

"I think you should," I say gently. "I think you're about ten years overdue."

His jaw tightens. "He shouldn't have let her go with them. You know that."

And it's back to Jennifer, the broken record that can't seem to leave our family's song. I glare at him. "He was fucking nineteen! And Jennifer's not coming back, whether the relationship between you two is intact or ruined. You know what she would have wanted." I pull at his arm and make him look me in the eye. "She would have wanted you to be close. To be what you used to be."

His shoulders drop. "I can't do it. I can't go back in there after the things I said. Just go find out what he's thinking. I called you here because I need you." His hand tightens on me. "We need you."

I can't deny that request. Not when it is the first time one of my brothers has reached out to me in years. I give him a final hug and then square my shoulders and clip toward the sliding glass doors, anxious to see my baby brother.

44

PAUL

I rest my head on her stomach, feeling the rise and fall of her chest and wonder how long they will let me stay. Will it be a doctor or my brother who will make me leave? I'm caught off guard when a soft female hand touches my arm.

"Hey." The woman tugs on my forearm.

I take a final breath of Madd's scent before I rise to follow the nurse.

But it isn't a nurse. I stared at her for a moment, confused. It's Dana.

I study her features, her cheeks pudgier, her eyes older, lips still dark red and pinched disapprovingly together. I haven't seen her in years. After Stewart's accusations and the guilt of Jennifer's death—I couldn't be around our family. Each interaction was a tainted reminder of the decision I made that killed her. And now Dana's here. A damn family reunion in the middle of Madd's hospital room.

My jaw tightens at the intrusion, but I can't help the wave of comfort and relief that pushed through me. Dana was our glue, our strength. She held us together until the point when everything fell apart. And in this fresh moment of hell, I want nothing more than to wrap my arms around her. "What are you doing here?"

She walks over to Madison and glances at the monitors. "Stewart called me. He explained the situation."

I make it to the chair beside her bed, and sink into it. "He blames it on me. Again."

She shakes her head. "No, he doesn't. That's his emotions talking. Same as it was with Jennifer. He's mad at the situation. You're just the closest thing for him to take his rage out on. Brush it off."

"I don't want to brush it off. It's bullshit. Bullshit that Madison doesn't need."

She tilts her head and studies me. "Don't speak for her. You want to speak up for yourself—fine. I think you should. I think you should tell Stewart everything that you've pent up over the last decade. I think you should tell him *exactly* how you feel about her, and exactly how you want this to end. He deserves you to verbally kick his ass, and he deserves to know how you feel about her. But it's a two-way street, and you need to be prepared to hear what he says."

"I heard what he said. He made it clear what he thinks of me."

"But do you know what he thinks of her?"

Her soft tone makes me pause, makes me consider my next words. "No. But I saw his reaction when he saw her. It... it wasn't what I would expect, knowing Stewart as I—we—once did." I look up to see her nodding, her mouth tight. "He loves her." The words rush out of me, words I've held back from myself, refusing to see what was so clearly laid out in devastating order before me.

She takes the seat to my left and reaches out, looping her fingers through mine. "I know," she whispers.

I lean into her, smelling smoke mixed with perfume, the scent different than what she used to wear. Her hair is now dark, a chocolate brown that suits her, and she's wearing a suit. I study the dark pinstripe of her pants. "What do I do, Dana? This whole thing is so fucked up."

"You talk to him." She pats my hand. "Go out and talk to him, away from her."

I shake my head. "I'm not leaving her. Not when any moment—" My words break. I swallow. "The doctor says she's still unstable."

She grips my arm tightly. "You don't need to fight over her body. Talk outside and give her a moment in peace to heal."

"No." I face her, hoping she'll see the resolve on my face. "Bring him here. She's as much a part of this as we are. I'm not leaving her side until they drag me away. Please."

Her body wilts a bit, and I can see disappointment in her eyes. "Fine." She lets go of my arm. "I'll go talk to him."

"Hey," I call out, a moment too late, as the door is swinging shut behind her. I make it to my feet and reach for the handle, but her foot kicks back, holding the door, and she raises her brows expectantly. "I missed you. Thanks for coming."

She steps backward, and I move forward, and we meet in a tight embrace that reminds me of what I've missed out on. "I love you," she whispers.

"I love you, too."

45

STEWART

I walk down the hall and the nurses barely glance up, the drama of earlier gone. They've now accepted the fact that Madison has two boyfriends, and that we are both present, the additional female regarded as a non-issue. I pocket my phone, ignoring the six new voicemails that all urgently demand a callback. They aren't important, yet are tapping on the back of my mind with annoying persistence.

Madison has never asked me to cut back my hours. She accepted my schedule, my obligations. She was fine with it, as long as we were non-exclusive.

I've always been exclusive to her. Partly out of necessity. Adding another factor to my life—either flings or consistent fucks—would be exhausting and unwarranted. And partly—most importantly—because I've never met a woman who compares to her. She got under my skin from the first moment I met her. I can't find that with anyone else, which is why I decided to propose to her on the breakneck drive to the hospital.

Change my life.

Make room for a marriage.

Move her higher up on the priority list.

A part of me wonders if I'll be able to cut back and work less. Delegate more?

Six voicemails.

Critical decisions need quick and decisive action. My current deals affect hundreds of employees, millions of dollars, and the futures of companies. I've never ignored calls or not returned voicemails, but I shouldn't—can't be thinking of them now.

I hesitate outside her door, taking a deep breath and steeling myself for the image of her, plugged in and supported with cords and machines. For the image of him, my baby brother with stars in his eyes and all grown up, ready to fight me over the woman I love.

I enter the room and his chin tilts up, his eyes steady on mine. He stands on the opposite side of her bed, and I step forward until the only thing separating us is her body. His eyes are damp but steady, and this is not the same man who crumbled under my words an hour earlier. This man has fight in his eyes, strength in his shoulders, and I am suddenly hit with a burst of pride in him.

We stare at each other for a long moment without speaking, two bulls squaring off for battle, the beat of her heartbeat a sick background harmony.

"You can't have her." His voice is strong, resolute.

I glance to the monitors. "Neither one of us might get that opportunity."

Anger lights his face. "She'll make it. You don't know her. She's strong."

I want to respond, to put him in his place, but the truth hits me hard. I *don't* know her. I know her body, every last inch of it. I can close my eyes and draw out every curve of her skin, freckle on her face, and flex of her muscles. I can tell from her breathing when she is about to come, can describe the moan she makes when she needs it harder, the gasp when my length has hit the place where she likes it. But her?

I've spent too little time with her. I love her, but I need more time to *know* her. I don't know what time she wakes up in the morning, don't know her favorite ice cream flavor, or what caused the small scar on the back of her knee. I don't know her mother's name, her favorite author, or how she likes her steak. But I do know that Paul is right. She has fire. She has fight. If there is a way, her mind will make it happen.

I move my gaze to her face, studying the details that peek out from the mask. "You love her."

"Yes. I'm not letting her go."

I pull my attention back to him, and wince at the resolve on his features. "You fall in love easily, Paul. You don't know what— "

"You don't know me anymore, Stewart. You don't have the right to tell me how I love. I'm not the nineteen-year-old kid you walked out on."

No, he isn't. I feel lost, like I have no footing in this room and am questioning every word that comes out of my mouth while he—he is so secure. Strong. Like this is his relationship, and I'm an intruder in it, instead of the other way around. "She was mine *first*, Paul. I had her. I told her to find someone to keep her entertained."

I met his gaze. "*Entertained*, Paul. That was it. I was always the primary in this relationship. You were the secondary."

"Your work is the primary. Everything else in your life comes secondary." His voice rises, and he jabs his finger toward me. "Tell me that isn't true. Tell me you didn't put her to the side while you slaved away for your job. Tell me she wasn't an afterthought to your business and deals."

I can't. I cover her hand with mine, wanting to get on my knees and beg for forgiveness. I hate him for being here right now when all I want is to be alone with her. I need to tell her how I feel, tell her the mistakes I've made, and apologize for any and every time I've put her second in my life.

I clear my throat. "I can't fix what I've done. I can only change going forward."

"Bullshit. You aren't going to step in as a Monday-morning quarterback. I gave her my heart almost two years ago, and have spent every day of that time being there for her. This is the woman I wake up next to every morning. I breathe and live for her. She's *mine*, despite whatever you think."

There is a soft cough behind me, and I turn to see Dana in the doorway. She crosses her arms and shoots us both a look. "I don't hear either one of you thinking about *her*. She doesn't *belong* to either of you. You're both acting like you hold any decision-making rights in her life, like you can fistfight your way to a victory. Who would *she* pick, if she was awake right now?"

I look away from Dana and down at Madison, focusing on the fragile rise and fall of her chest.

I am absolutely terrified of that answer.

46

DANA

I don't know what to make of my brothers and the men they have become. They snarl and snap over her silent body like she is the last scrap of meat, and they are starving. They're both desperate in their love and both terrified of losing her. Both reckless in their announcement of happily ever after. But they're forgetting the most important thing in this clusterfuck: they don't have much of a choice. If she does wake up, this will be her choice to make.

I'm torn over this woman and my feelings for her. I've spent the last two months hating her as I secretly tried to figure out her motives and evil plan. And now, it appears she has no plan at all. Stewart was the executor of this insane figure eight. Madison is just the center of it, the place where the two halves come together and meet.

This entire situation is a disaster, and it's at this terrible moment that the slow beeping that has been the heartbeat of this horror show slows, the change in tempo catching all of our attention. Lights that I never noticed begin to flash, alarms begin to sound, and all I can focus on is the beeping has stopped.

Stopped.

Flatline.

Both men rush forward as the door slams open and white coats swarm.

47

MADISON

I cannot speak for others who have died. Their experiences might have been different. They might have been met at glittery gates by Morgan Freeman and cute little cherubs with cheeks of sparkles. I only know that it felt like being pulled. Not forward in a vacuum of suck, but pulled apart, each arm and limb yanked slowly, an excruciating pain as cracks formed in bones, tissues and muscles popped and ripped. My chest attempted to pump as ventricles broke loose and cavities collapsed. My heart struggled to pick a side as my body broke in half, tearing down the middle in an unclean division of all the things that made my body whole. Its pieces were stubborn, sewn into ribcages and sternums, and finally yanked into two separate pieces, my soul screaming in protest as I was released to the heavens.

48

PAUL

There is shouting, unintelligible words, a blur of coats and we are
pushed aside, the small room suddenly full, my back hitting the
sharp edge of a machine. I struggle to see her face, my panicked
eyes meeting Stewart's, despair in his blue eyes. Our gaze holds for
a moment, and in that moment, everything is forgiven. We need
only one thing, and I return my gaze to her body, which is so still,
the monitor still showing a flat line, buzzing and alarms echoing
throughout the room. I choke back a sob and press a fist against my
mouth as promises spill out of me. I promise things I will never be
able to deliver, promise to let her go, to let her be with him. I
promise to lead a perfect life, to devote myself to good, anything,
everything, just to have her live. I need her life. I cannot, will not,
make it without her. I don't have to have her as mine, but I need
her to live.

This world cannot lose her. I cannot exist if she is not alive.

49

STEWART

Six voicemails.

The fact that it crosses my mind in this moment is sickening, and something I will never admit to anyone. I push it out of my mind the moment it creeps in, desperate to bury it with emotions, love, grief, anything.

I don't deserve her. I don't deserve anything but my empty office, stacked with deadlines and trades, dotted lines and P&Ls. I don't deserve the sunny smile flirting with me while snow dots her face, her giggle when I awaken her at four AM, her hand tugging me to my feet while she drops to her knees. I try to catch sight of her, try to see past the flash of metal, white cloth, and gloves. I try to see her face. I try to send her a silent apology for every piece of the man that I am not. I step backward, against the wall, and pray for forgiveness.

50

DANA

There are too many people in the room, all with a purpose or a deep-ingrained love that will not allow their feet to move. I'm the only one who doesn't belong. I'm the outsider, watching the train wreck with a morbid fascination.

I can't help them. This is something they have to figure out amongst themselves. I don't envy Madison when she wakes up. Survival of death should be a celebration, but instead, it will be a tense, who-will-you-choose, tug of war. She will wake to expectant eyes, competing affections, and pregnant pauses. I need to protect her. I need to keep their competition at bay and allow her to heal. I am suddenly struck with the irony of those thoughts. For months, I have been worried about protecting them from her. And now, now that I am actually in the discussion, I've crawled over the fence and now guard the opposite side.

As the flatline stretches out, her body jerks with electricity from the paddles, and I realize I may not even have a fence to protect.

51

MADISON

I am brought back to life at 4:08 PM. It is with a jarring impact, my back slamming against the bed with a hard thunk. My eyes flip open to bright white light, shining intensely down on me, heads breaking the line of white, hands everywhere, touching, lifting, squeezing my skin. I briefly hear Paul's voice, then my eyes close, and I sink back into darkness.

I am so, so, tired.

I feel a squeeze then a release. A squeeze and then a release. A hum of sounds, a familiar cadence that my brain recognizes as speech—the words unintelligible. I struggle, the grip on my hand tightening as I try to move. I open my eyes, crust sticking my lashes together, and I blink to clear them.

An unfamiliar face peers into mine—the man's features studied, his eyes sharp, looking carefully into mine. I frown, trying to place him, trying to place the white tile ceiling behind his head. *Where am I?* There's a roar in my head, spots appearing in my vision, and I wince, closing my eyes briefly, the peace instantly returning, and I relax against the pillow, grateful for the reprieve.

The hand squeezes again, and the voices return, incessant and irritating. I try to pull my hand away, try to roll to my side and block out the voices. I want to sleep, and this party of people are putting a cramp in that style.

It won't stop, and now a second hand has joined in, squeezing my other hand. I groan, opening my eyes again, the white glare doing the tango in stilettos on my head, shooting needles straight into my temples. I try and focus, try to move my mouth and tell these persistent assholes to go to hell. I can't move my head, can't do anything but stare up into the light, and I wonder where the stranger went, if he is still here, if he is one of the damn people squeezing my hands to death. A new face enters my vision, and I relax slightly. Paul.

He leans forward, speaking so loudly that someone two blocks away could hear, the angle of his approach revealing that he is one of the hand squeezers. "Madd, can you hear me?"

I blink at him and try to speak. Swallow and try again, the words coming out as a whisper. "I'm not deaf. Please... shut up and let me sleep."

He grins. The damn man grins, a smile that stretches across his face as if he has just won the Mavericks Invitational. "Yes, baby," he whispers, and I would swear that a tear leaks from his eyes.

"Thank you," I grumble, my voice coming out hoarse, my eyes closing against the still-brutal light. "And please have someone turn that damn light off."

"Anything else, babe?" His voice is close to my ear but at a normal decibel level, and I can feel the warm tickle of breath against my eardrum.

"Yeah." I sigh, the glare against the darks of my eyelids gone, some angel having found the fry light, turning it off. "Stop strangling my hands."

If he responds, I don't hear it. Darkness is once again my new best friend.

52

DANA

I find Stewart in one of the lobby chairs, his fingers busy on his phone. He looks up at my approach. "Hey sis."

"She's asleep but stable. You didn't want to stay in the room?"

He shakes his head, and I can see the defeat in every line of his posture.

I sit next to him and run my hand over his shoulder, picking a bit of lint off of the material. "It's okay that she didn't see you when she woke up. She'll know you were here. Chances are, she won't even remember it."

He shakes his head. "It doesn't matter. The point wasn't for her to see me. I'm just glad I saw it." He lets out a breath of air. "God, when her eyes opened, when I heard her voice... it was a weight off my shoulders. I've never been so scared, Dana. I mean, with Jennifer, there was never an unknown period. We were just told what happened and had to deal with it in any way we could. With

Madison and the unknown, the waiting..." He turns to look at me. "I was terrified."

His shoulders sag, as if there's no strength in his bones, his body drained of any energy or hope. And in his eyes, there's disappointment. I don't understand it. "You should go in there. She might wake back up."

His expression darkens. "No. I want Paul... God, I don't know." He leans forward in his chair and rests his forearms on his knees, staring down at his shoes. "I don't think..." he says carefully, and every word is measured in preciosity, "that I deserve her."

"In what way?"

He rubs his lips with the tip of his fingers. "I don't think I can do it, D." He looks back at me. "And I wouldn't tell another soul but you this. The work—the job—I don't know that I can walk from it or cut back my hours to a level she would expect. Deserve." He sighs, and I hate the self-loathing in his eyes. "Fuck, I can't even sit in a hospital room while she struggles for life and not think about work." He looks away. "Paul, he doesn't struggle with that. She's all he's thinking about. If I told him to walk away from surfing tomorrow to be with her, you know what?" He raises his hand in frustration. "He'd do it. Wouldn't hesitate a second." He looks at me. "Am I right?"

Of course, he is. I can see his mind ticking, and his speech continues without waiting for my response.

"She's all that he loves in life." His shoulders sag. "Do I have the right to take that from him? And then fail her later?" He runs a hand through his hair, gripping the short strands before dropping his head. "So where does that leave me? A life alone, with nothing but my work? She's..." his voice breaks. "She's the only thing I have other than that."

I grab his knee and squeeze it hard until he looks at me. "I know stepping away from her seems difficult. But if she is truly the woman for you, you wouldn't have to try and cut back your hours. You wouldn't struggle to balance your time. You wouldn't be able to stay away from her. When *that* time comes, *that's* when you'll know that you have found the person you're meant to be with. When your life is no longer your own, and you are pushing forward that sacrifice willingly." I rub my right temple. "Though it won't be a sacrifice then. If that makes any sense."

He holds my gaze for a long moment before glancing towards the ICU doors. "So, you think that is how Paul feels? You think she is *it* for him?"

I follow his glance, flipping back through everything I've seen today. "I don't know," I say carefully. "I think you and I both still see Paul as he once was—emotional and tender-hearted. But he's ten years older now. He's not the teenager we once knew. And the *only* thing on his mind in there is her. He... he's not like anything I would've expected. It terrifies me how singularly focused he is on her. It's as if he thinks he can will and love her back to health."

He groans. "God, you make me feel like shit, D."

I lean against his shoulder and loop my arm through his. "You're sacrificing a piece of your life for him. This is the proudest I've ever been of you." I catch the slight curl of his mouth in my peripheral vision.

"I haven't made a decision, Dana."

"Yes, you have," I say firmly. "Now go outside and make your calls. I'll tell Paul." I stand, brushing off my pants and reach for my purse.

He reaches out and stops me. "I love her." The raw need in his eyes makes me pause, and a spike of pain hits my heart.

"I know," I say softly. "But you also love him."

His jaw tightens.

53

MADISON

Kisses. Soft brushes of lips against my cheeks, nose, and gently moving down my neck. I shift slightly, bending toward the contact, and slowly open my eyes. Everything is blurry, the room dark. The kisses find their way to my lips, and I smile, recognizing the soft way he cradles my head. "Hey baby."

"Hey." Paul kisses my forehead. "How do you feel?"

"Okay." My head aches. "What time is it?"

"Almost ten. In about five minutes their most intimidating nurse is going to come in and try and kick me out. Just in case she succeeds, I wanted to say hi." He presses a button and the lamp beside my bed comes on.

"Hi," I say weakly, and he smiles. He looks bad, my Paul. It's the way he looks when he comes back from a two-week stint in Australia—a little gaunt and underfed, desperate for my touch and starved for my company.

"What happened?" I glance around the room, and hiss at the

blinding slice of pain that stabs my temple. I lift up my hand and gingerly touch my head. I'm shocked at the bare skin, a portion of my head shaved.

"You wiped out. The board came back and hit you on the head."

"I'm in the hospital for that?" I find a bandage, and trace my fingers around the edge of it.

His face tightens. "You were without oxygen for a while. And with head trauma... for a while we didn't think you'd make it."

"We?"

His eyes hold mine. "The doctors ... and also Stewart. He was here."

My heart sinks in my chest. "Here?" *With you?* A volley of unspoken thoughts screams through my mind.

"Yeah." He clears his throat. "But don't worry about that now. You need to rest."

"Is he here now?"

"No. He left a few hours ago, once your condition stabilized."

"And how long will you stay?" I wanted to grab his hand, to squeeze it, but every moment was making my head pain worse.

He gives me a rueful smile. "Until they drag me away."

I close my eyes as another burst of pain lights every receptor in my brain. "My head hurts," I mumble.

I hear him stand and his hand brushes over my bare head, placing a soft kiss on my forehead. "I'll get the nurse," he whispers.

I keep my eyes closed and wait for the pain to ease, the process not helped by my racing thoughts. Stewart was *here*. With Paul. In the same room. Speaking. Interacting. I'm almost grateful I was unconscious. What had been said? What conversations were had? Had there been a fight?

With a different man, I would wonder at his absence, and what it meant to our relationship, but this is Stewart. His work, no doubt, needed attention. I'm surprised he stayed until I gained consciousness.

I open my eyes and notice the flowers, big arrangements stacked along the opposite wall of the private room. I think of my relationships.

This is the moment. The collision of lives. Yet it's so quiet. So peaceful. I've been steeling myself for this moment, expecting to have to choose which of my men I love the most. But maybe, with hours of unknown events having passed... maybe that choice has been taken from me. And in *that* light, Stewart's absence seems more notable.

The door swings open and a nurse scurries in, clipboard in hand. "You're awake!" she says with a beam. She picks up a remote and presses it into my palm. "This is painkiller. Just press this button if the discomfort gets too strong. I'm adding a bit into your IV, so I wouldn't be surprised if you fall back asleep pretty soon."

I nod, and place the remote on my stomach, my gaze finding Paul's. He gives me a worried smile and turns to the nurse. "How do her vitals look?"

"Good. We're moving in the right direction, and we'll monitor her closely tonight." She pats my arm, and I attempt a smile, the pain already less.

"How long was I out?" Each word hurts, the expelled air scraping out of my raw throat.

She glances at my chart. "About twelve hours."

Twelve hours. Cities burn to the ground in less time than that. I wait for her to leave and watch as Paul carefully sits on the edge of my bed. The door clicks behind her, and I wet my lips.

"What happened with Stewart?" I have to know.

"He had work to do." He glances at my face. "He'll probably be back tomorrow."

Probably. I can see the pain in his eyes, and it suddenly strikes me that I've never seen him this way. He's worried.

He moves aside the blanket, exposing my hand, and squeezes it. Helplessness consumes me. I need to get out of this bed. I want to comfort him, to push that darkness from his eyes. I want to find Stewart, to make him look me in my eyes and ask him what he is thinking. I kick my feet out and a fissure of pain rockets through my skull. I gasp, spots dotting across my vision, and carefully settle back against the pillow.

"What's wrong? Do you need the nurse?" He leans over me, his grip tight on my hand, and I manage to shake my head.

I envision Stewart, his head turning to me, our gazes meeting. "Tell me what you are thinking!" I would shout. But I'd be disappointed in the answer. I close my eyes and my vision of him spins, his mouth moving, quoting figures and emails, contracts and legal mumbo jumbo that I don't understand. He lifts his phone to his ear and I watch as his hands fly over the keys.

"Madd, are you okay?"

I wet my tongue. "Fine." I find the remote with my free hand and jab at the button. "Tired."

He presses a kiss to my cheek and falls silent. I pinch my eyes shut against the tears.

—

I wake once to voices, arguing softly. Paul and a nurse. The second time I wake, the room is dark, the faded outline of Paul in a recliner, a white blanket stretched over his large frame, the size too small to cover his feet. I let my eyes adjust to the room, the pain present enough for me to reach for the remote, press the button on its front.

I am grateful for the silence. For the ability to think without being observed.

I've lived in this fairytale for so long, it is hard to imagine an alternative. But this feels like the time. The time to pick a path and move forward. I look at the man asleep next to me. It is no surprise that he's here, that he won the battle against the nurse to sleep beside me. He's always been here for me. He's my rock, no matter what kind of crazy quasi-relationship we've had for the last two years.

I let out a painful breath and think of Stewart. Also, not a surprise that he is absent. Our entire relationship has been squeezed in between stretches of absence. His passion for work is one of the things I love about him, but it has always been a competing piece— the fourth person in this triangle. And I've always known where I stood in that order—behind that passion, peering over its shoulder and waving my hands for attention.

At this juncture, the decision should be easy. Paul is right here, just waiting for a shot at my entire heart. He's been waiting for it ever since that day under the pier. I was just too distracted by Stewart, too emotionally tied to him, to see Paul in the role he should have been in.

It should be easy, but it's not. The decision hurts, yet I know that it's the right one.

I reach out for him, then clear my throat, coughing slightly, and Paul instantly moves, his hand swinging out and hitting the wall. He trips over the foot of the recliner and stands, his body tense, listening in the darkness. I softly say his name, and he comes forward, gently reaching out until his hands find my bed.

"Are you okay, Madd? Do you need the nurse?"

"I'm fine," I whisper. "I just... Paul. I just wanted to say that I love you."

He pauses, stiffening. "I love you too, baby," he says gruffly, kneeling beside my bed and holding my hand. "God, I love you so much."

"Forever and always," I whisper.

He surprises me by crawling into the bed, the narrow width barely able to accommodate us both. He moves cords and lines with heart-breaking tenderness, turning me carefully on my side and wrapping his arm around me. I relax, my lids heavy. At this moment in time, there is not a more perfect place I could imagine. Not another man on Earth who I want holding me.

"Forever and always," Paul whispers.

I close my eyes and push back a stab of guilt.

54

DANA

I wake two hours early, rolling out of bed with a purpose. It is the first day in almost a decade that I have my boys back. Thanks, in no small part, to Madison. The same Madison who I, in a brief moment of creativity, dart-boarded last week after too many margaritas. But that was before. Before she almost died, and Stewart called me, and I got to hug Paul and look into both of their eyes. Before I found out that she wasn't running their hearts through a shredder for her personal enjoyment. I almost, just a teeny bit, feel some affection for the woman.

I dress for work, putting on a red suit and black sling-backs, and pull my hair into a low bun. Leaving my contacts in their case, I stick with glasses and minimal makeup, jogging out the door at 5:45 AM with two bananas and an apple in my purse and a giant mug of coffee in my hand.

Sixteen minutes later, I step through the hospital doors and smile brightly at the receptionist. Three minutes later, I'm escorted to her room.

"She will still be asleep," the silver-haired woman explained in a hushed voice. "But you can sit in there until she wakes up. Her notes say she was coherent and speaking late last night."

Late last night. That would have been after Stewart left, his phone already to his ear. Hopefully, Paul was here. By the look on his face, he had had no intentions of going anywhere. I gently press on the door and tiptoe inside.

My heart swoons when I see them. A tall frame hugging her small body, both of them crammed into a narrow space that should be uncomfortable but looks perfect. His head is nestled in her hair, his arm across her body. Her eyes are closed, a small smile on her face, her feet tucked in between his legs. I hesitate in the doorway, then step backward, pulling the door gently closed.

I make my way back to the receptionist area and veer right, following the path to the cafeteria, and pull my cell from my pocket as I walk. I dial Stewart.

"Hey."

"Hey. I'm at the hospital. Just wanted to check and see if you were coming by."

He sighs, heavy into the phone. "I can't now. I have..." There is the rustle of papers, and I hear him speaking to someone else. Then he is back. "Is she stable?"

"Yes." I can't stop the smile from entering my voice. "The nurse said she had a good night. They haven't woken her yet this morning."

He exhales loudly into the receiver. "That's so great, Dana. That... God, I can't describe how that makes me feel. Have you told Paul?"

"He stayed the night." I wait to see his reaction, and there's a long stretch of silence before he speaks.

"That's good. I'm glad someone was there when she woke up. Do you know if she asked for me?"

"I don't know. But today, she'll need to know the connection between you two. She won't understand otherwise."

His voice is suddenly abrupt. "I know. Just handle it however you think best. Let her know, if she asks, that I love her."

"You love her." I wait a moment. "That's it?"

"That's all I can do," he says quietly. "She'll understand. It's one of the things I love about her."

He ends the call, and his statements echo in my head. *I love her. One of the things I love about her.* The silly grin, one I'd been wearing since I walked in and saw Paul cuddling with her, drops.

I sit in an uneven chair and eat rubbery eggs, staring at the Los Angeles Times and trying to think. I woke up delusional, thinking this would all turn out easy. I'd envisioned a scenario where Stewart would walk away without looking back and leave Paul to his happiness. I didn't factor in the fact that he still loves her, that emotions don't have an off switch.

God, I knew that better than anyone. I still pine for my ex-husband, who's happy as a pig in shit with his new wife. Who was I to think that Stewart could, with one simple chitchat with me, wash his hands of any emotion?

I take a sip of coffee and watch the clock tick. I need to get to work. It's tax time, with a deadline approaching that can't be missed. But I don't know my younger brother well enough to trust that he'll handle this correctly. Hell, *I* don't even know how to handle it correctly.

It's one giant ball of screwed up. Paul is ecstatic at the fact that she's alive. Joyous at the fact that he might have her all to himself. Stewart is brooding in his office of solitude, still tossing out emotions like shedding skin, the fresh new skin just as love-affected as what is falling off. I'm being greedy, like an underfed vulture, swooping down, excited about the carnage and what it could mean for me.

And the woman who it all centers around—she's the biggest unknown. How does she feel? Who does she want? Stewart has stepped away, but what if she chases him? What if she *chooses* him? Paul... I can't imagine what that would do to him.

I push back from the table and carry my tray to the trash, accidentally dumping my fork in. I watch as the metal utensil slides down into a mountain of yuck. I debate reaching for it, then glance around casually. No one is looking and I stack the tray on top and heft my purse over my shoulder, heading back to her room.

I turn a corner and almost run into Paul, his hair messy, a white V-neck paired with bright yellow board shorts. An apology tumbles out, then stops. A smile breaks over his face when he realizes that it's me. God, I've missed his smile, that dimple in his cheek, his carefree eyes, the sparkle in them when he is happy.

"Hey sis." He wraps his arms around me, squashing my purse to my chest in one tight embrace. "Did you hear? She's awake." He releases me, stepping back. "She's back—just like before. No damage."

I smile at him. "I heard. The nurse told me. I was just coming to you now."

"The nurse is cleaning her up now—but I know she'll want to meet you. Can you stick around for a bit?"

I hesitate, hating to dampen his smile. "You need to tell her about you and Stewart."

He scowls, and the look instantly takes me back in time. Him, six years old, mad over a broken toy. Him, eleven years old, pouting when I refused to let him surf in a storm. "Stewart's gone. Why does it matter?"

"Stewart will never be gone, Paul. He's your brother. She needs to know that—needs to have all the facts so that she can understand the situation and make the right decision."

"Decision?" Panic flares in his eyes. "You told me yesterday Stewart was stepping back. Letting her go. She loves *me*."

"You can't start a relationship with a secret. Let me talk to her. Explain everything. Allow her to come to grips with it."

He leans against the wall and crosses his arms, his features tight. "I don't want to lose her, D."

I nod. "I know."

"She'll choose me." He nods, and I can see him trying to convince himself of the fact. Glancing at me, he raised one brow. "Right?"

I meet his uncertain gaze. "I don't know her, Paul. But I know Stewart isn't at a place in his life where he can fully commit to a relationship. And I'm sure she knows that."

His face darkened. "I don't want her to choose me because she can't have him. I want her to choose me because I'm who she wants. I want..." he ran his hands roughly through his hair. "*Fuck.* I want her to be happy."

I move closer and squeeze his arm. "Let me talk to her. The brother thing is going to be a lot for her to take. Go get some breakfast and give us some time."

He doesn't move, staring straight ahead, and I leave him there, my heels clicking along the linoleum floor, my mind sorting through how to break this news to a stranger.

55

MADISON

The nurse pats my arm with a smile, her brown eyes warm and friendly. "I'll be back in an hour to check on you. Press the button if you feel any pain."

"When can I go home?" My throat is still on fire, and the words come out scratchy and raw.

She wrinkles her brow. "It'll be a few days, but the doctor can give you a better timeline than me."

"I feel fine now." It's a lie. My head's killing me, I feel bouts of nausea, and every breath feels like I'm rubbing sandpaper down my throat, but I'm anxious to leave. I've only been conscious for an hour, and I'm already sick of this place. I want my bed, the sound of waves, and the smell of salt air. I want Paul's arms around me, his kisses against my skin, a warm mug of his lemon tea.

"We still need to monitor you for a while. You've pulled out strong, but with the brain, nothing is certain." She smiles to soften her words and grabs my chart, maneuvering around someone as she exits. I look up, expecting Paul, and am surprised by the tall woman who enters, dressed in a red suit, her outfit out of place in this world of white. She moves confidently into the room, her eyes on mine, and extends an arm, my own raising out of habit. As I shake her hand, I wonder who she is. An insurance rep? Hospital adminis-trator? Her face is familiar, and I study it, trying to place where I have seen her.

"I apologize for coming in so early, but I wanted to introduce myself. My name is Dana. I'm Paul's sister."

I blink at her in surprise, my hand falling limply to the bed as she releases it. I struggle to play a frantic game of catch-up. Sister?

I swallow painfully, my mind piecing together the little that Paul has shared about his past. "Sister? I thought that..."

She grimaces, her expression pained. "You're thinking of Jennifer. She passed away when Paul was a teenager."

"A car accident."

"Yes. I'm his older sister. I was at college when that happened. Paul probably hasn't mentioned me—he cut all contact with the family when she died."

I nod, a faint recollection of a second sister entering my head. Paul has always been so dismissive in discussing his family, the still-raw pain of his sister's death causing some degree of anger, his reason for the separation from his family not given. It's the one area of his life we don't discuss, the topic turning my cheerful love into a brooding, depressed man. Early in our relationship, I pushed the issue, thinking he needed to talk about it. But it put him in such a dark place that, ever since then, I've avoided the subject.

"Is Paul aware that you're here?" I ask carefully, trying to under-stand her presence.

"Yes, I was here last night." She smiles. "We've reconnected, something I am grateful to you for." Her face pales, and she covers her mouth. "That sounds horrible—I didn't mean—"

I wave her off with a weak smile. "I understood what you meant. I'm glad that you are on good terms again. Family is important."

Her face stills, and she squares her shoulders. "Yes. And *that* is why I needed to speak to you."

I tense at the look on her face. Something is coming, from a stranger whose name Paul hasn't even mentioned in the last two years. I suddenly wish I'd pressed him harder over the reason for their strife.

She doesn't mince words or cushion the situation. "I am the oldest of three. Paul is my youngest brother. Stewart—*your* Stewart—is my other brother. Paul and Stewart are brothers, but have been estranged for almost a decade."

I study her eyes, noting that they are brown and not the brilliant blue of my boys. My brain, still sluggish, wonders where the brown came from, if it was the paternal or maternal gene that produced that color. Would my babies with Paul have icy blue or chocolate brown eyes? Her gaze sharpens and I realize she's waiting for something. A reaction. I flip back through her words, piecing the sentences together, the structure unnecessarily complicated, the final words sharpening into focus, my brain comprehending the situation in one, delayed moment. *Brothers.*

I control my features and struggle to choose the proper response, whatever it is that this woman wants me to say. I find none.

I'm in love with brothers. My unwinnable situation is more fucked up than original perception led you to believe. I still love them just as much, my attraction almost more understandable now that the reasons for their similarities are known. I swallow, and try to speak, try to say something that this woman will respect.

"What do you suggest I do?"

It isn't the reaction she expects and she flinches in surprise. "Me? I'm not involved in your relationships. I just wanted you to know the reason that Stewart—"

"... is leaving me." I finish the sentence for her. Lying back on the bed, I look up at the ceiling. It's not a surprise. Circumstances dictated him to choose between a full-time relationship and a full-time commitment to work, and work won. It's his obsession, his passion. I was his release, his outlet. I know he loves me. I never doubted that fact. And I was okay being second, because I had Paul. Paul, who has never placed anything before me. Paul, who would put down his surfboard in a moment if I asked him. And I briefly consider that Paul played a role in Stewart's decision to walk away. Had I lost him purely to his work? Or had his family also been a factor?

I hoped, for whatever reason, that Paul was part of the motivation for Stewart's decision.

"Yes. It's not that he doesn't care for you—"

I turn to her and lift my hand, stopping her worried attempt. "I know. You don't have to explain. Stewart's work is who he is. Paul being brought into the situation makes the decision easy for him."

She looks at me carefully, and I can see the confusion in her eyes. "So... you're fine with this."

I swallow, folding over the hem of the blanket. "This situation has always had an end date. In a way, I've been preparing for this for a long time. The fact that they're brothers..." My voice fails for a moment, and I reach for the glass of water, taking a sip before continuing. "Stewart's relationship with Paul is more important. Have they spoken?"

She nods. "They haven't reconciled, but I think it's possible. They've both held a lot of anger toward each other for the last ten years, and I think this situation... it's caused them to let that go.

Not that Stewart really has time for family, but..." She smiles. "Paul is feeling very grateful to Stewart right now."

"For me."

"Yes." She looks at me with the same direct stare that Stewart uses, one that seems to peer into my soul and strangle the truth from me. "Is that who *you* want? Paul?"

I sigh. "I've asked myself for two years which one of them I would choose—if put in that situation. I love Paul. I love our life together. We fit in a way that's easy. Seamless." I can feel my hand start to tremble and I slip it under the blanket. "Stewart is the opposite of me. He gives me a different side to life. I'll miss that part, that intensity, that fire. But just because I'll miss it doesn't mean it's meant to be my every day. I don't know if I could *handle* him every day. And I would never be happy with being second to his work. And I could never ask him to work less. You know him. His work... it's his breath. He has a fire for it, it's what makes him tick."

I reach up to run my left hand through my hair, then flinch when I realize that it is gone. "I don't know if I would have ever willingly walked away from Stewart—but this is what's best. I know that. I love Paul. It wasn't really ever fair for any of us—what was going on." I blink, realizing suddenly that tears are welling, and embarrassment seeps through me at the weakness. I wipe at my eyes, avoiding her gaze. "I just want him to be happy," I whisper. "I hate the thought of him being alone."

Her arms wrap around me, and the strength of them is comforting. I relax in her embrace and let the tears, and the guilt, flow.

Stewart never came back to the hospital. Every time the door opened, or I heard a voice in the hall, I expected it to be him. But he never returned.

They release me a week later, at a point where I'm trying to rip the IV from my arm and biting the heads off anyone but Paul or Dana.

I finally realized where I recognized Dana from, and her face turned bright red when I brought it up. Over hospital Jello and shit coffee, we laughed over that afternoon at the bookstore, and she told me the truth. How she'd watched me. Suspected me of some master plan. How she hated me from afar. She apologized, though none was needed, and we'd hugged. And then she paid me the nicest compliment I'd ever gotten.

"I see why they love you. It's hard, while in your presence, not to love you."

I'd blushed and taken a sip of coffee to disguise the reaction, thinking about how vile I'd been since waking up. How she was able to see any redeeming qualities was a shock.

But today, finally, they put me in a wheelchair and take me out to Paul's Jeep, parked at the curb. The wheelchair is unnecessary; I could have cartwheeled out of there. But some hospital policy requires it, and I'm only too happy to oblige. Anything to speed my exit. Anything to get me out of the sterile environment and back into beach air and sun.

Paul lifts me from the chair despite my protests, taking advantage of the act and brushing his lips over mine. "I love you, Maddy."

I grin at him. "I love you, too."

"I'm so happy you're coming home."

I don't know if he is referring to my near-death experience, or the fact that I am now fully his, without a second man hovering over our relationship. But either way, I'm happy, too. More than happy. I'm anxious for our new life together. And yet, there the guilt is. Leaning onto my shoulder and whispering in my ear. Every smile, every burst of happiness seems to be quickly accompanied by a twinge of guilt. I'm coming home to Paul. I'm making a life with him. Stewart will be alone. *Twinge.*

Paul sets me in the front seat and buckles the belt around me, his normal scent of ocean and sunscreen replaced by hand sanitizer and ivory soap. I'm suddenly anxious for us to swim. To wash away all of the last four days and literally dive back into our old world.

"Paul," I say softly, and his head turns quickly at the words.

"Yes? What's wrong, are you in pain?"

I smile to appease his worry. "No. When we get home, I want to go down to the beach. Just to see the water for a moment." *To smell it. To taste it on the air.*

He smiles and leans forward to give me another kiss. "If that's what you want. I'll do anything you want."

Anything. It's true. The last two years have taught me that. *Anything.* It's a heavy word when used correctly. A word that can hold unknown possibilities.

56

VENICE BEACH, CA

It is good to be back. To step from the jeep and walk on my own. I stretch in our carport before turning to Paul, seeing him round the Jeep, his gaze intently examining me, looking for some sign of physical weakness. I grin and shoot him a look he knows, a look that leads to ditched clothes and feverous hands. He returns the smile, relief crossing his features, and reaches for me.

I awkwardly dip around him, dropping my bag on the concrete, and make it into the sunshine outside our garage. "Uh-uh," I click my tongue at him. "Ocean—now."

"I want *you*, now," he growls, stepping out of the darkness, his hand catching my sundress and tugging on the fabric until I am against him. "Seeing as you seem to be back to normal."

I grab his hand and tug him along the alley. "First, the water."

He wraps an arm around me and presses soft kisses on my head as we walk down a broken sidewalk we have traveled countless times before. A block from the water, when we round a corner and see the glint of afternoon sun reflecting off the waves, he bends, catching me off guard, and swoops me into his arms, smiling down at me as he moves.

"I don't want you to trip in the sand," he explains.

"Uh-huh," I tease. I twist and point to the water. "Take me in."

His gaze moves to my bandage, and I roll my eyes.

"Not underwater. Just a little bit."

"It's cold out," he warns. "Are you sure you're up for it?"

"If I'm too heavy just say so."

His hands tighten on me and he tilts back his head and laughs. Such a beautiful sound, and paired with that huge smile I have missed. My heart tugs and I inhale the salt air deeply, beaming out of pure joy. He walks toward the water, smiling down at me, and I can almost see the stress as it leaves his body. He pulls me to him for a kiss, then carefully wades into the water.

"Sure you want to get wet?" he warns.

My hands tighten around his neck as a gust of cool air blows across the water, sending a spray of water against my side. "Never mind." I shake my head to free a wet strand of hair and take another deep breath. "This is enough. I just missed it."

He kisses the top of my head. "I know. Me too."

A wave approaches and he steps back, stumbling a little until we reach firm sand. There, he carefully lowers me to my feet. Someone from the water calls out my name and I turn to see a group of surfers wave, a chorus of hands moving above bright boards. I wave back, then laugh when the surf hits, another blast of spray coating my yoga pants and T-shirt.

Paul tugs at my hand. "How 'bout you let me take you inside? Let the shower warm us up?"

"Or something else." I smile suggestively.

"Or something else." He grins, and I squeeze his hand tighter.

57

VENICE BEACH, CA

The house is just as I remember it, and I feel a burst of shock at how much has changed in our world since I last walked through these doors.

"Come here," he whispers, adjusting the thermostat before leading me into our bedroom and pulling me close. He rubs his hands over my arms and steals a quick kiss as he yanks at his shorts and drops them to the floor.

Wow. Anyone who thinks water causes shrinkage has never met this man. At least, not this man at this moment in time. He is, despite the smile he shoots me, raring to go, and I am suddenly warm, my skin tingling, the heat between us erasing anything else.

"Turn around, baby." His words are soft, but I hear their directive and meet his eyes, a curl of pleasure shooting through me at the look in them. Raw need. A fire burning behind his cocky smile. This is the Paul I know, the one who expresses love best through touch, and who can barely contain his emotions in this moment.

I turn, hearing him blow into his hands, feeling the warmth of his skin as he pulls at my shirt, his hands gently lifting the damp material off, his fingers lingering on me as they trail down my arm, as if they want every bit of me they can get. He carefully tugs at my pants, pulling them slowly down, his breath hot on my back as he exhales against my skin, planting a soft wet kiss there, my panties the next victim to his sure and unhurried movement.

He stays close to me, unclasping my bra, his hands sliding down my back and then curving around my sides, slipping under the loose cups and cupping my breasts, squeezing them, pulling my body back against his chest, the hot line of his arousal hitting the top of my ass, my body greedy for more contact against his skin. He kisses my neck from behind, whispering my name as his hands explore my front, running over the lines of my stomach, the curve of my breasts, the hard tips of my nipples. I am suddenly needy for him in ways I have never been, needing to know that this is real, that he is mine, and we have made it through this experience intact, the proof of it hard against my backside, and I want it, him, now, in every way that I can have him. His touch slides lower, and I moan, pushing my ass back against him as his hands gently cup me, his mouth taking a delicious line across the hollows of my neck.

"Madd, I never … you have no idea how much I love you," he groans, grinding against me, his hands holding me in place as he pushes the hard ridge of himself antagonizingly close to where I need it.

"Please," I whisper. "Paul, I need to feel it. I need you inside of me."

"In a minute, baby." Instead, I feel his fingers, their gentle exploration over and across my sex, and I push against him, groaning when they finally move inside, slowly sliding in and out, their maddening length and width not enough for what I need.

I moan, my legs weakening from the delicious touch. "Please," I beg.

He rasps, his voice thick at the nape of my neck, his arm wrapping around and hugging me to his chest. "Tell me, Madd. Tell me that you need me."

"I do," I pant. "I do. Please. Give it to me." My legs buckle as he crooks his fingers, brushing them back and forth over my pleasure spot.

"Only me," he says firmly, brushing his digits in a way that makes me moan. "Come to the thought of my cock," he whispers. "Then I'll show you exactly what it can do."

I do. I push every lingering thought of Stewart out of my head, physically feel as they leave my body, and focus on Paul—my love—focus on the stiff head of him that is sliding between my legs, inches from where I need it most, so hard that it is sticking straight out. I close my eyes and think about every time he has made me moan, how his face looks when he loses control, the fire in his eyes when he watches me come. The images take me

over the edge...

back arching...

stars forming...

pleasure ripping tingling paths through my body...

Paul's fingers keep up the rhythm, the perfect pressure and tickle across my g-spot, every swipe bringing new life into my orgasm, until I finally sink back against his chest. I look over my shoulder and into his eyes, my drugged vision putting him in a haze of gorgeous blue eyes and five o'clock shadows.

"Fuck me," I croak, and his eyes darken, a devious smile of carnal possibilities sweeping across his gorgeous face.

"We have to be careful," he warns, moving me forward, until we are both on the bed and I am on my back and he is opening up my thighs. "Tell me if anything hurts."

"It won't." I bring my knees up and watch as he positions himself at my entrance, then lowers his chest to mine. He shifts his hips and my mouth opens in a silent O of pleasure as he pushes inside. "Please, Paul... I need you."

"Tell me," he says softly, slowly pumping the head of his cock in and out, short half strokes that feel amazing, the ridge of his head scraping back and forth over my G-spot. "Tell me how you want it."

"Hard," I whisper, my arousal knotting and expanding in anticipation of what is to come. He gives one hard thrust and then returns to his motion, his short quick strokes torturously perfect. A gasp, followed by a moan, spills out of my mouth and I reach back and grip the bars of our headboard tightly, digging my heels into him and fighting the urge to slam my hips against his pelvis and impale myself on his cock.

"Are you mine?" His voice is tight, guttural, and I smile despite myself, his pace increasing, his attempt to be gentle getting lost in the heat of the moment. My nipples brush like hard pebbles across his chest and our eyes meet as he rocks on top of me.

"Answer me," he demands, and I hear the hoarse edge of desperation, his need for confirmation. His short and controlled thrusts are taking me closer and closer, the intensity building in my core, and my thoughts become delirious from the sensation.

"All yours, Paul. There is no one else. I—oh God—love you." The words tear from my mouth as my pussy clenches, my orgasm hovering and then breaking. It is then, while my world caves in, while I am mindlessly oblivious to anything but my own ecstasy, that he stops using the head of his dick and shoves fully in.

Fullness. The long, hard ridge of him inside me, branding me as his own, his need as desperate as mine. He doesn't ease into the rhythm, doesn't give either of us time to react. He just dominates me: hard, firm fucks that bury inside with every stroke, a furious rhythm of domination, his breath fast and loud, my name ripping from his lips as he takes me as his own.

I am going to come again, the shaking of my body, the animalistic fever of Paul, a man unleashed, the level of his possession so fucking hot.

"Tell me, Madd," he gasps. "Tell me that you are mine."

I can't. I can't respond because my eyes are too tightly shut, my body racking underneath him, pushing harder, greedier against his skin, needing every stroke, every fuck, every inch of his thick cock as I come, a bundling outpour of muscles flexing and contracting, a scream coming from my throat, his hands loosening as I release the sound, my body growing rigid, his fucks continuing, his own climax close.

When I come up for air, I tell him. I tell him how I have always loved him. How he has always had my heart. How now, he will be the only one in it. I look up at him, at his beautiful face, hair mussed, eyes vulnerable as he meets my eyes, relief spilling into those blue depths of perfection. He suddenly slows his strokes, the moment changing, and rolls me over, pulling out long enough to lift me above him. He kisses me deeply, murmuring soft words of love as he grips my waist and lowers me onto him, slowly and carefully, his eyes on mine.

It feels so different without Stewart. It feels, in ways, like the first time we've ever made love, like every other time was a threesome with an invisible presence watching over us. Now, as I bend over him, as I lean down and kiss his lips, I feel his relief. I feel an absence of fear, and I realize how unfair I've been to him. I realize how every experience must have seemed a competition, every visit I took to Hollywood prompting worry in him that I might not return. His palm settles over my heart, his touch shaky, as if he is unsure if I'm really here and feels the need to have to verify it for himself.

I wrap my hands around his neck, lower my mouth to his. And I tell him, in between kisses, how deeply I love him. How I will never leave. How I am his for as long as he will have me.

His hands tighten, his kisses deepen, then he closes his eyes, thrusts deep, and comes.

58

VENICE BEACH, CA

The effects of drowning are not long-term. Head injury is a fickle bitch; it can sneak back up and knock you on your ass when you least expect it. But there is no reason for bed rest and no reason Paul has taken a month off surfing to wait on me. But... I'm not gonna complain. I want the worry to fade from his eyes. To him, my death is still too real of a possibility. Time will be the only thing to disquiet his concern.

We sit on the couch with my feet in his hands, his fingers gently rubbing across my soles, and it takes a moment to react when my cell rings. I glance at the display, my chest tightening when I see Stewart's name. I changed his contact name the day I returned home, the act of deleting LOVER and replacing it with his name cathartic in the transformation.

I wasn't sure if he'd call. Part of me has feared he'd drop in, every car engine causing my muscles to tighten with nerves. I show Paul the screen, and he squeezes my feet, moving them off his lap, and stands, bending over quickly and dropping a kiss on my cheek. "I'll run out, grab groceries, let you talk."

Our eyes meet, unsaid communication flowing through them, and I thank God that I know him so well. It is all there, in the slight tightening of his shoulders, in his quick and easy smile that hides so much. *Talk to him. Make sure you are making the right decision. Come back to me. I need you. I love you. I am better for you.*

I reassure him with my eyes, then answer the phone, hearing the jingle of keys and then the firm, complete shut of the door. *Come back to me.*

"Hey babe." The voice is Stewart's, but the strain in his words is that of a stranger.

My raw throat abandons me, my own words scratchy and weak. "Hey."

"I'm sorry I never saw you at the hospital. I was there—until you stabilized. I just, Paul..." He exhales, and I can picture him at his desk, papers stacked around him, his hand working through his hair as he flexes his handsome jaw. "The whole thing caught me so off guard. I should have stayed— "

"You did the right thing." He did. I don't know what I would have done if they had both hovered over me, pulled me in between, and fought over me.

"I love you. You know that."

I feel the sudden urge to cry. The push of emotion surges in my throat, and I know my next breath will be a gasp. A shuddering, yes-I'm-crying, gasp. I cover the mouthpiece and press my mouth into the pillow of the couch, choking back a sob against the leather.

He's waiting, his declaration hanging out there, and I've given him nothing but silence in response.

"I just feel ..." There is a voice in the background, then muffled conversation, the scratchy thud of skin against the mouthpiece, and I blink back tears as I hear bits of a very familiar exchange.

I know, before he even returns to the phone, what his next words will be. *I just feel* ... Do I even want to know the rest of that sentence? Do I want to know how he feels? Or will it be the final tear that rips my barely-held-together heart?

"Madison, I'm sorry. I—"

"... have to go." I finish the sentence for him and feel the drip of undeserved tears as they run down my cheeks. I clear my throat, needing to say something before he leaves, hoping he will wait long enough to hear them. "Stewart—one last thing."

One last thing. Three casual words that suddenly scream of finality. I swallow the weakness and strive for a clear tone. "I've loved Paul for a long time. I think... we would have ended up here anyway." *I choose Paul.* "You leaving the hospital, you giving us this opportunity..." I clear my throat. "Thank you."

"If you change your mind—I'm here. You know that."

"I know." *No, you're not there. Pieces of you not consumed by work are there. You have never been there.*

There is a moment of silence and then he hangs up the phone. I drop the phone on the couch, hug the pillow to my chest and let out the sob.

59

HOLLYWOOD, CA

STEWART

I take my hand off the phone's hook, the receiver still against my ear, and listen to the drone of the dial tone, my thoughts somewhere else, my mind shaky from the sound of her voice. The door to the office flies open, and Ashley's frame barges in.

"We need you *now*, Mr. Brand. Conference Room Four. Everyone is waiting."

I move the receiver away from my ear, waving a hand dismissively at her, and set it in the cradle. "No need for that. She's gone."

She comes to a stop, her eyes on mine, and her voice drops in pitch and volume. "Are you okay?"

I sigh, the thick exhale rumbling through my throat and run my hand slowly over the top of the desk, feeling the grain of wood beneath my fingers. "I—" the words drop, and I clear my throat, start again. "I fear I have made a mistake."

She takes a moment and sits on the arm of a chair, ignoring the statement and moving on to her own inquisition. "Why'd you have me cut off the call? Why didn't you talk to her longer?"

I meet her gaze, needing the frank directness of her stare. "Honestly? I was worried what I might say."

"You walk away from big deals all of the time."

"She's not a deal." The words roll harshly off my tongue, and she meets my glare without hesitation.

"That's how you treated her, Stewart. And that's why she never committed to you. You didn't *just* make this decision. You've made it every day I've worked for you. You're right. You have made a mistake. But it wasn't a week ago. It was two years ago. Celebrate that you've finally walked away from it." She stands, her eyes flashing, and sets the folder she was carrying on the desk. "And my second interruption wasn't an act. You have people waiting in the conference room."

I sit back in my chair as she slams the door, listening to the irritated clip of her heels fading down the hall. I close my eyes and think of Madison's grin in the dark of my bedroom. Her hands tugging me closer. The way her laugh releases the tension in my chest.

There, alone in my office, I take a moment and mourn my mistakes.

60

ONE YEAR LATER

SMUGGLING: [VERB]

TO HIDE AROUSAL, USUALLY BY HOLDING YOUR BOARD
IN FRONT OF YOU WHILE WALKING.

There are ways you shouldn't think about your future brother-in-law. Places that should be off-limits for your mind to wander. Like right now. I am watching his hand skim down the open back of her dress, slipping inside and gripping her waist, his thumb rubbing a soft pattern on her skin. My eyes can't pull from that spot, from the slow motion of his hand, the seductive pass over her skin. I know how that feels, know how frantic he gets when he fucks, how he pushes deep with his cock, pins you to the mattress, or the desk, or the floor, his hands hard on your wrists, his face intense above you, heat and raw need in his eyes. I blink and turn away, looking for Dana. Her strength grounds me and her knowledge of everything we've been through reassures me.

ALESSANDRA TORRE

She smiles at me from the kitchen, waving me over with a flour-covered hand. "I need those fingers. Come knead this dough."

I wash my hands in the small island sink and pat them dry on a sunflower hand towel, joining her at the counter, diving into the sticky dough, grateful for the job.

"How's it going?" she murmurs.

"Fine," I say softly, though no one is close enough to hear. "I've only spoken to him once—when he introduced me to her."

"And ..." She takes a handful of flour and sprinkles a line of it on the counter. "What do you think of her?"

I consider the best way to word my response. "I think..." I pause to scratch my forearm. "She's nice. Accommodating. Stewart says she's a web designer?"

She snorts. "That's putting it lightly. She created a site that just signed a deal with Apple."

So the quiet blonde is successful and smart. I wait for the flow of jealousy to poke its green head up, but instead, a smile forms. I've spent so much of the last year feeling guilty. My life with Paul has been wonderful—perfect. But every bit of happiness has felt slightly tainted by the fact that Stewart was alone, left out in the cold as Paul and I continued full-steam ahead in our happy relationship. And now, with our engagement, I'm terrified of how Stewart will react. Could the brothers' new, fragile relationship weather the announcement?

Seeing Stewart show up with a date had lifted that guilt and sent a spike of relief through me. He'll be okay. We'll be okay. I believed it, and I desperately hoped it was the truth.

Arms slip around me, gripping my waist and pulling me back. I turn my head and catch a soft kiss in the crook of my neck. "Stop," I giggle. "The bread!"

"The bread can wait," Paul says softly, spinning me around and delivering an innocent kiss that deepens into something more, his pelvis dipping into me, my belly curling at the contact. I moan against his mouth.

"Wow." Dana smacks Paul's shoulder with the spoon. "Point made. You guys can melt each other's clothes off. I got two bedrooms upstairs should you feel the need for more." She stares pointedly at Paul. "Now *'git*, Loverboy. Go back and tend to the steaks and let me have some time with her."

He grins at her and steals one last kiss. "I love you, baby."

"I love you, too," I whisper, glancing around quickly before shooing him away. "Now go, before Stewart comes back."

"He's too gaga over his date to notice anything," he says, his relief matching my own.

Dana shoves Paul aside. "That's it. Outside. You get all night with her, give me a measly fifteen minutes." She points to the back door, her expression firm, and he sends me a playful smile before heading outside.

She shoots me an exasperated look. "Please tell me he's not like that all the time."

I bite back a smile. "Okay."

She pulls out a pan and unwraps a stick of butter, spreading it around the base. "So... you hiding that ring for a reason?"

I glance toward the living room, the muted voices alerting me of Stewart's presence. "You know why."

"Uh-huh." She moved to the sink, turning on the water to wash her hands. "You scared?"

"I'm nervous. It'll be our first conversation in person, since the accident. Paul wanted to tell him, but this is important to me. I need this conversation with him."

She nodded. "I agree. It was one of the reasons I invited everyone over. That, and I've been itching for a family Thanksgiving since I bought this house." She grins. "No other point in having a twelve-person dining room set."

I try to return the smile, but at the thought of speaking to Stewart, my stomach twists into knots.

The Thanksgiving meal is a success, the table filled with turkey, ham, and enough side items to feed a family three times our size. We eat our fill and then abandon the dishes and move to the den. I stand in the doorway and watch Stewart. I've never known him to have time for sports. Frankly, I'm surprised he even knows how football works. But right now, his arm is around her and his attention is on the game. I tap his shoulder gently, and he looks up at me.

"Could I speak to you for a minute?" I smile awkwardly at Mia. "I won't keep him long, I promise."

He squeezes her shoulder. "I'll be right back." She nods, giving me a tight smile and turns back to the game. She hasn't exactly been friendly to me, but I can't blame her for that. If she knows anything about this situation at all, she probably thinks I'm the world's biggest slut.

Stewart holds the back door open, and we step outside, my skin standing at attention in the cool fall air. I shiver slightly, and his eyes sharpen on the movement, his movement visibly restrained when he starts to move forward and stops. We both laugh, and the awkwardness breaks. "Want to sit on the steps?" he offers.

"That sounds great."

We sit, his long legs stretching down the steps, and I struggle with where to begin. Do I dive into the engagement first? Ask about work? Mia? That orchid I kept in our bathroom?

He glances over at me, his gaze moving over my face, as if he's memorizing the features. "I've missed you."

I look away, focusing on the house behind Dana's. They're hanging Christmas lights, a ladder propped up against the brick, a string half-strung across the eves. "I've missed you, too. We had some good times."

He chuckles. "Yeah. Most of our good times involved very little clothing."

Color floods my cheeks, and I grin at the truth in his statement. "Yeah."

"I'm sorry I didn't call again. To follow up after the accident."

The somber tone of his voice surprises me, and I shake off the apology. "You had work. You always have work. I understood that—that's how your life is."

"I'll always love you, Madison," he says quietly, and my heart tugged at the words. "I love you for mending this family and for making Paul happy. But the *in love with you* part... I've moved on from that and I'm really happy for you, for both of you."

I have to look over at him then, have to risk my heart to see if he is telling the truth. He meets my gaze and gives me a rueful and unfamiliar smile, one I can't read but want desperately to believe. *He still loves me, but he's not in love with me.* It's the best-case scenario, and I reach out and wrap my arms around him, burying my face in his shirt as I hug him.

"Hey, there." He squeezes me and I don't realize I'm crying until he pulls back and wipes at the top of my cheeks.

"They're happy tears," I swear. "Honestly."

"I've never seen you cry before." He sounds surprised at the realization and I pause, my emotions tapered as I consider the possibility.

"Are you sure? Never?" I think of sad movies, but we never watched movies together. I think of serious conversations, but we rarely had any. We never fought, or had injuries, or dove into painful memories. He hadn't seen me cry, and I'd never seen him cry. I blinked at the realization of exactly how superficial our relationship must have been.

I notice him studying me, his handsome features pinched in concentration.

"We're gonna be okay, right?"

"Yes." I force a smile. "We have to be. We're gonna be stuck together for a while." I hesitate, then step toward the edge. "In fact, that was one of the things I wanted to talk to you about."

"What's wrong? What is it?"

I jump off the cliff. "Nothing's wrong. Paul proposed."

The reaction comes slowly, but it appears, a wide grin that splits his face in an almost unnatural way. A *grin*. Stewart... doesn't really grin. Not normally. He scowls, he glints, but *grinning*? It's such an odd look that I stare at him in surprise. He grabs my hand and his smile drops when he sees my bare finger. "You said no?"

I shake my head with a smile. "No, I accepted. I just didn't want to show up wearing a ring, not without talking to you about it first."

He pulls me into a hug, one so tight that I squeak.

"So, you're fine with this?" I push out of the hug, wanting to see his eyes.

"You'll be my sister now, Madison. As totally creepy as that is, seeing as I still got a raging hard-on when you walked in the house—"

"Shut up," I choke out, blushing at my own inappropriate thoughts.

"Seriously," he says. "You'll always be in my life now. That couldn't make me happier. And Paul—he loves you so much. More than I did. He deserves you, Madd."

"Madd? You've never called me that before." I wrinkle my nose at him.

He shrugs. "Things are different now."

"So, we have your blessing?"

He wraps an arm around my neck and places a quick kiss on my forehead. "More than that, babe. You have my heart. Both of you." He releases me and stands, holding out a hand to help me up.

"Did he get you a good ring?" he asks gruffly.

I nod with a smile. "He did good. You'd approve."

And Paul *had* done well. It wasn't a Stewart ring, one picked out by his assistant that shouted my status while begging me to be mugged. But for Paul and me, it was perfect. A blue sapphire, the color of the ocean after a storm, framed by tiny diamonds.

Paul had surprised me with the ring on a Sunday morning. I'd been wrapped in a big blanket, the ocean air whistling through the cracked window. Paul had handed me a mug of coffee, and I waited for him to sit behind me and cradle me back against his chest. It was how we often spent the lazy mornings that didn't involve early morning surfing or sex. Instead, he'd dropped to one knee, his eyes tight to mine, his hands fumbling as he opened the box and extended it. He'd choked out the question, his voice tight, his hands shaking, his gaze glued to mine. And I'd sat there for one shocked moment before my mind responded, and I'd launched myself into his arms, covering him with kisses and chanting the word *yes*.

He had been so worried, so nervous that I would say no. But he'd had nothing to worry about. I've always been his. I've loved him since the moment I saw his playful grin in a line at Santa Monica Pier, his eyes studying me as I took the place next to him. And finally, with my relationship status one devastating blue-eyed brother less, we had nothing holding us back.

I return to Dana's den, and watch as Stewart pulls Paul into a congratulatory hug, their faces holding matching, dimpled grins. I watch them closely, but there is no sign of tension or competition in the air. It's incredible that this train wreck ended in such a perfect fashion. My boys, the ones I fought so long to keep separate, are embracing. I get to keep them both in my life. I've emerged with my heart intact and get to continue life with the man I love. The man who, from the beginning, has waited patiently for this chance.

I cross to him, his gorgeous face beaming as he collapses on the couch and pulls me onto his lap. I lean back against his chest and look into his eyes.

Their eyes should have been my first clue. Piercing blue, too gorgeous, and too unique to be a coincidence. But this man's eyes... they see into my soul. They know every bit of me, and accept it all. I will grow old with this man. I will have his babies and teach them to surf. And I'll try, through it all, to be worthy of his love.

EPILOGUE

GLASSY: [adjective]: smooth seas resulting from calm wind conditions, little disruption, nothing hidden beneath the surface

---

I knew. I'd known for a long time. Since I'd opened our mailbox one day and saw Paul's real last name. Not the one he'd used for as long as I'd known him, the one plastered over surfer magazines and endorsement deals. I'd known he used a pseudonym, one for the press, but I'd never taken the time to dig deeper. Paul Linx was how I knew him, was how he lived his everyday life. But that day, on the broken concrete that led to our garage, I flipped through envelopes and stopped at one with a different last name. Paul Brand. A unique last name. So unique it made my hand shake, the mail scattering on the ground. I told myself it was probably a coincidence. A crazy, highly unlikely coincidence. As crazy and highly unlikely as dating two men who end up being related.

Then, all of the similarities between them flooded my mind.

Piercing blue eyes. A kissable curved mouth. Rugged features. Tall, athletic builds. Even the impressiveness that hung between their legs. *Jesus*. Both of them, estranged from their families. Both who had—at some point in time—mentioned a brother. I had been stupid for not seeing the possibility sooner.

I'd scooped up the mail, stumbled upstairs, and had a full-blown panic attack. I'd sat on the couch and counted to ten, then twenty, then one hundred, breathing deep, ragged gasps of air, my mind racing with the implications.

At the time, it had seemed disastrous. Insurmountable. Right then, right at that moment, I would have to choose. I had to pick. There was no going around it.

But it was too late. My heart had gone too far, jumped over two cliffs and plummeted past the point of return. I couldn't do it. I couldn't willingly rip a piece of my heart off and flush it down the toilet. I'd have to break up with one of them with no way to explain the reason. I couldn't. I couldn't throw a bomb into this perfect world where everything was flowing so well, smiles all around, orgasms at every turn.

So, I didn't do anything at all. I left the mail on the counter, and went about my life the same as before. But I made sure to keep my lives separate. Made sure to never mention their names or details of our separate lives. Not that the boys noticed. They were blissfully ignorant of each other and happy about it. So I lived the life, knowing the entire time that there was an expiration date. Knowing that one day the truth would come out and our perfect world would implode.

I dreaded that implosion for so long. Stressed over it, worried over what disasters it would bring. But now? I roll over in bed and burrow against Paul, who wraps his arms around me, pulling me close, and gently presses his lips to my forehead. I think I knew all along how this would probably end.

Deepak Chopra once said: "All great changes are preceded by chaos." Looking back, chaos was a great way to describe our lives. I saw it as perfection, only because I didn't know what could exist, what lay on the other side. Now? Now that I know? I am grateful for the chaos. Grateful for the immense change that it brought. Grateful that now, I'm in a pleasant state of calm.

Note From Author: I originally published this book in 2013. Since that time, Stewart has continued to nag at me. I think he needs his happy ending, and am currently plotting out a way for him to fall in love. If you'd like to read his book, please click here and I'll email you once this novel is written. I'll do my best to publish it in 2019.

NOTE FROM THE AUTHOR

WHEW! This book was a rollercoaster to write. I had a huge block about 60% in, when I kept wringing my hands and screaming 'I don't know who to choose!'. Yes, Paul won. Which is funny, because I had always expected her to end up with Stewart. But my characters rarely behave, which is one reason why I love them so much.

If you are interested in reading more of my books, please visit my website, or consider following me on Facebook or Instagram. If you avoid social networks, my monthly newsletter is a great way to enter giveaways and get sneak peeks at upcoming books. You can join my newsletter at nextnovel.com.

I do have an *extra special* bonus scene – if you are feeling frisky, please visit alessandratorre.com/secretfantasy/ - and enjoy! Warning: It's sexy!

Made in the USA
Las Vegas, NV
04 July 2021